# THE MAJOR AND
# THE MINERS

# THE MAJOR AND THE MINERS

### LEONARD MEARES

A Black Horse Western

ROBERT HALE · LONDON

© Leonard Meares 1992
First published in Great Britain 1992

ISBN 0 7090 4968 4

Robert Hale Limited
Clerkenwell House
Clerkenwell Green
London EC1R 0HT

Photoset in North Wales by
Derek Doyle & Associates, Mold, Clwyd.
Printed in Great Britain by
St Edmundsbury Press Ltd, Bury St Edmunds, Suffolk.
Bound by WBC Bookbinders Ltd, Bridgend, Mid-Glamorgan.

# 1

# Trouble Down South

The mayor of Shayville, Southeast Colorado, was a long way from home. At the establishment of the Quinn Brothers, 60, Aurora Street, Denver, tonsorial consultants to the gentry of the state's capital, he was having his hair trimmed by Ernie Quinn.

Ben Leeson was overburdened by problems at this time, big ones. He was slight of build, sharp-featured and passably well-groomed.

'Noticed the sign in your window,' he remarked, as Ernie Quinn clipped and snipped. 'Braddock Detective Agency.'

'Our tenants, sir,' said Quinn. 'Nice couple. Sure, Rick Braddock's a smart detective, gets results.'

'Would he be up there right now? Would I need to make an appointment?'

'Need a detective, huh?'

'It might take a special investigator to do what I want done. The state administrators aren't interested in my problems. For all the help they are, I could've saved myself the long journey from where I came from.'

'His wife'll be up there if Rick isn't. She's his partner.'

Leeson was taken aback.

'A lady detective?'

'Smart as Rick himself. Any man underestimates Hattie Braddock – big mistake. *Big* mistake.'

After being talcummed and brushed down, Leeson paid for his haircut, added a modest tip and decided he *should* consult a special investigator. Was he not desperate? Damn it, desperate was an understatement.

Emerging from the barber shop, he moved along to the flight of wooden steps and climbed to the door bearing the inscription BRADDOCK DETECTIVE AGENCY. He knocked and, a few moments later, the door was opened by a young woman in a simple cotton gown, the garment favoured by the typical housewife. On her, it could have been a Paris model. She was beautiful of face and figure, a blue-eyed blonde whose smile bedazzled him; he had to remind himself he was old enough to be her father and that he still loved his wife.

'Good morning,' she greeted. 'You wish to consult my husband? I'm Harriet Braddock.'

'Uh – Leeson, ma'am. Mayor Benjamin Leeson of Shayville. And – yes – if Mister Braddock's free …'

'Resting, Mayor Leeson. So busy of late, you understand, so many cases. But do come in.'

She ushered him into the room that did double service as parlour and office, seated him by a table and made for the bedroom. Entering, she closed the door behind her and moved across to perch on the edge of the bed. Prone and perusing the latest edition of the Denver *Leader* was her handsome, dark-haired husband, a six-footer five years her senior. Horizontal and in his shirtsleeves, he didn't appear as muscular, as leather-tough as his loving wife knew him to be.

'Baseball at Compton Park tomorrow, big game,' he told her. 'If I can find a bookie, I might lay a bet on the Denver Cougars.'

'How about business?' she smiled.

'Business is slack.'

'Might be picking up, darling.'

'We have a client?'

'Could have. His name's Ben Leeson and he's mayor of a town I never heard of. Shayville.'

'Looks worried?'

'Very.'

'They're the best kind.' Rick rose from the bed and began donning his coat. 'Go ahead, spouse. Give him the pitch, then I'll make my entrance.'

'Once a ham, always a ham,' she teased.

'Listen to who's talking,' he grinned.

'Point taken,' she shrugged, and left the room to rejoin the prospective client.

Show business. It would always be in their blood. The Braddocks were probably the most versatile couple in the state of Colorado. Before meeting and marrying, they had roughed it, getting by as best they could, orphans of the frontier, but never babes in the wood. At the tender age of sixteen, Rick was already an experienced prospector and ranch-hand, also a wily gambler. He was self-taught in Spanish with a smattering of French and several Indian dialects, could play several musical instruments and had travelled with carnivals and repertory groups during which time he had honed his skills as a character actor. And he knew guns. Name any firearm; he was proficient.

Hattie's girlhood and early womanhood had been just as varied. After losing her parents, a schoolmaster and a music-teacher, to pneumonia, she had gone it alone, turning her hand to any means of making a living, hustling dishes in hashhouses, nursemaiding, working as a seamstress and then, as Rick had done, joining one tent show after another. Kooch dancer, chorus girl, assistant to knife-throwers and magicians; she had done it all, including playing every female role in travelling theatre groups, sometimes ingenues, sometimes even grandmotherly types. When it came to make-up and character parts, she was as skilled as her husband. So now they were more than a happy married couple; they were a partnership.

'My husband will be with us presently,' she informed Leeson, seating herself and reaching for pad and pencil. 'I will, as usual, take notes.'

Leeson was impressed, and even more so when Rick strode in, offering an amiable grin and a strong hand. As they shook, he identified himself.

'Rickard James Braddock, Mayor Leeson, at your service. You've met my wife.' He sank into his chair. 'And now to business. You have a problem. Tell us about it. One point at a time, if you please.'

Leeson did his best. He tended to ramble, but the Braddocks listened intently, getting the gist of it all.

Shayville's mayor, they learned, had full confidence in that mining town's law officers, Sheriff Vin Strother and his deputies, Roy Bass and Billy Grimble. So did the majority of the townsfolk, but the miners of the Shay Ridge diggings, some of them independents, most of them employees of Elias Jacklin, owner-manager of Jacklin Mineral Enterprises, were an unruly lot. They tended to raise hell when visiting the county seat. Nevertheless, Strother and his aides kept busy, kept them under control to the satisfaction of Leeson and his fellow-aldermen. However ...

'We got three banks in Shayville,' grouched the mayor. 'And the bankers're real bluenoses, them and their wives. Last time we had trouble – some woman got molested and I recall there was a street fight too – those stuffshirts panicked and went over our heads, ignored the town council and petitioned the state authorities.'

'Demanded Federal marshals be brought in,' Rick assumed.

'Worse than that,' sighed Leeson. 'You see, there'd been some looting and killing. Ever hear of Bearcat Webster?'

'I've heard of Quanah Parker,' frowned Rick.

'Webster's a half-breed like Parker,' said Leeson. 'Half-Arapaho. Savvies plenty English. A dangerous renegade, and that's putting it mild. Got a secret camp somewhere, him and a bunch of renegades he's organized, about three dozen of 'em. There was this isolated claim along the ridge called the Lucky Seven. Well, those seven prospectors ran out of luck the day Bearcat and his warriors raided 'em. Only one survivor, feller name of Arnfield. Those renegades got away with about eight leather sacks of nuggets, the pure stuff, and left Arnfield for dead. Poor feller'll live, but he'll be lame the rest of his life.'

'So,' prodded Rick. 'After that disaster, the bankers petitioned the state government.'

'For army protection,' groaned Leeson. 'And those government big shots obliged. Same old story, Mister Braddock. The government, state or Federal, always obliges bankers. Money talks. So now my town's under martial law. From Camp Kemp, headquarters of the Third Colorado Cavalry, a whole company of troopers was sent to keep the peace in my town. The officer in charge is Major Calvin Royle, and he's a

horse's neck and a real pain in the butt.' He loosed a
shocked gasp, held hand to mouth and gawked
contritely at Hattie. 'Ma'am, I sure beg your pardon!'

With a sweet smile, Hattie suggested,

'An apology may not be called for. Please tell us
more about the major.'

'I never met a man so all-fired conceited,' complained Leeson. 'He's a blowhard and he's pushy. His
Shayville billet is the Grand Hotel. He just moved
himself and a lot of troopers in and took over, and now
Chloe – she's my wife – Chloe and I are living in a
rented house. And I *own* the Grand Hotel! Major
Royle acts like he's king of Shayville. He's in charge of
everything and Vin Strother and his deputies got no
authority at all.'

'So no apology required, Mayor Leeson.' Hattie
made a note. 'Quite obviously, Major Royle *is* a pain in
the butt.'

Leeson blinked at her, then at Rick, who calmly
explained, 'Mrs Braddock is a lady to her fingertips,
but also a realist.'

'Mister Braddock, you're a lucky man,' Leeson said
with fervour.

'By contrast, sir, your luck is running low,' Rick
sympathized. 'Please continue.'

Martial law in Shayville had worsened an already
difficult situation, as far as the citizens were concerned. The troopers could not be called guardians of
the peace. They were as rough and as wayward as
off-duty minehands, swaggering tearaways and
womanizers. Shayville's distaff side feared them as
much as they feared slobbering prospectors, and with
good reason. Far from improving, conditions were
becoming intolerable. The respectable women of the
town were no longer safe on the streets – day or night.

'Fine soldiers, I don't think,' scowled the mayor. 'We call 'em Royle's Roughnecks.'

'Catchy,' commented Hattie.

'Major Royle is showing little consideration for the citizens it seems,' said Rick.

'He hates us, and I'll tell you why,' muttered Leeson. 'Right after that massacre at the Lucky Seven claim, something mighty important was stolen from the armoury at Camp Kemp. A quartermaster sergeant and a trooper were butchered – it had to be Bearcat Webster's dirty work – and a gun stolen, and it's never been recovered.'

'Just one gun?' asked Rick.

'Listen, I'm not talking about a rifle or a pistol,' declared Leeson. 'They got away with a Gatling and three full magazines for it!'

Hattie winced. Rick whistled softly.

'That *is* trouble,' he said. 'A Gatling in the hands of renegade Indians. Do you happen to know if …?'

'It was the Third Cavalry's only Gatling,' said Leeson.

'A winding trigger mechanism,' mused Rick. 'The Gatling throws fifty calibre rounds at great speed. If Custer'd had the foresight to take just two of them along, the battle of the Little Bighorn would've gone the other way.'

'Major Royle's got a fool notion it was civilians disguised as Indians who hijacked the big gun,' Leeson said bitterly. 'Every other day or so, that pompous showoff orders a house-to-house search. We get troopers tramping through our homes – can you beat that?'

'How did that foolish man ever attain the rank of major?' wondered Hattie. 'Could he be related to a member of the chiefs of staff?'

'I'm starting to believe most of his relatives are in institutions,' Rick said scathingly. 'There has been a lot of inbreeding, I suspect.' He nodded to the mayor of Shayville — wherever the hell Shayville was. 'Specifically, what are you asking of me?'

'Well,' said Leeson. 'I was thinking — uh — what we need most is to be free of martial law. We want Royle and his troopers out of our town and back at the cavalry headquarters where they belong. So we have to prove we don't need 'em.'

'That's logical,' Rick agreed.

'And the only way we'll do that is to clean up our own backyard,' opined Leeson. 'Those rowdies, the minehands and troopers, have to be straightened out — Royle too. I don't know how it can be done. I mean they're all investigating the Lucky Seven raid and the theft of the Gatling, but getting nowhere. So I thought — uh — somebody from outside, a detective, a smarter investigator, might get to the bottom of the whole lousy mess.' He added, persuasively, 'The county treasury'd guarantee your fee, you can be sure of that. So what do you say?'

Though he had already decided, as had his wife, Rick pretended to deliberate.

'No run-of-the-mill assignment, Mayor Leeson. And I don't come cheap.'

'Name your price,' urged Leeson.

The Braddocks had a comfortable bank balance at this time, mostly due to Rick's luck at Denver's best gambling houses. He liked Ben Leeson, so decided to cut his rates.

'Twenty-five dollars a day, plus expenses,' he announced.

Leeson responded by producing his wallet and laying a $50 bill on the table.

'Something on account,' he said. 'How soon can you start?'

'When are you returning to Shayville?' demanded Rick.

'I'm booked on the afternoon southbound, Wells Fargo,' said Leeson.

'I'll be on tomorrow's southbound,' Rick told him.

'And I'll leave day after tomorrow,' offered Hattie.

'You're both gonna …?' began Leeson.

'The feminine touch can be very useful,' Rick said. 'We often collaborate.' He nodded to the banknote. 'Hattie, my dear, please write a receipt while I explain what'll be expected of our client.'

'There's something *I* have to do?' challenged Leeson.

'There most certainly is, sir.' Rick spoke quietly, but forcefully. 'It's imperative we maintain absolute secrecy. If by chance you do recognize either of us in Shayville, you will not greet us, you will pretend you never saw us before.'

'*If* I recognize you?' frowned Leeson.

'It's just as likely you won't,' said Rick.

'We'll be in disguise,' explained Hattie, handing Leeson the receipt. 'In our profession, we refer to this type of assignment as an undercover operation.'

'If I need to contact you, it'll be done discreetly,' Rick assured him.

'Well, sure, fine.' Leeson rose to leave. 'And I shouldn't ask how you'll do – whatever you intend doing, huh?'

'We couldn't tell you anyway,' said Rick. 'It depends on circumstances. After familiarizing ourselves with the local scene, we may have to improvise. In our line of work, that's how we function, taking everything as it comes, one step at a time.'

Leeson shook his hand, aimed a last admiring glance at Hattie and departed. The Braddocks stood studying each other thoughtfully.

'In over our heads, do you think?' frowned Hattie.

'It's complicated,' he reflected.

'Rick, darling, it's a *mess*,' she declared.

'I'd work this case for free, if only because of that damn Gatling,' he muttered. 'Half-breeds like this Webster are the most dangerous renegades of all. With such a weapon, he could block a charge by the entire Third Cavalry – and there'd be heavy casualties. Honey, I can't stay out of this one.'

'Getting near lunchtime,' she said, and retreated to the kitchen.

He joined her there, drawing out a chair, straddling it and resting his arms on its back, watching her at the stove.

'Every move you make, even the humdrum routine of rustling up a meal,' he observed. 'So graceful. A joy to the eye.'

'You're ogling me.'

'The gold band on your third finger left hand is a symbol of my right to ogle.'

'So ogle on, dear heart.'

Later, over lunch, he asked,

'Any ideas about your disguise?'

'I'm open to suggestions from my favourite adviser.'

'Well, there's no guessing whether or not older ladies go unmolested in a town like Shayville, but let's cling to that hope.'

Hattie was eating sedately.

'So I'll be a dear old soul, fifty or thereabouts. I can manage that easily enough.' On one point, she was adamant. 'But I refuse to use that pillow under my dress routine, pretending to be in an advanced state of pregnancy. It was too uncomfortable that other time. So much for my disguise. How about you?'

'Pretty much the same,' he decided. 'I always preferred character roles anyway.'

'Padding?' she asked.

'Not rightaway,' he said. 'Not unless I have to assume a second identity while I'm there. I think, for openers, I'll get along by adding thirty years to my age.'

'How about protection?' she demanded.

'I'll keep the Colt in my grip at the start,' he said. 'The Smith and Wesson thirty-eight with the cut-down barrel is less conspicuous, fits snugly in the armpit holster.'

'We'd better agree on aliases.'

'Fairchild has a good sound to it. Yes, I'll be Julius Fairchild. And stop giggling.'

'Julius!'

'Your turn. Come on now. If I can pull a name out of thin air, so can you.'

'I think I'll present myself as a genteel widow. How does Mrs Elmira Tebbut sound?'

'Genteel as all get-out. Reminiscent of lavender, old lace and whalebone corsets.'

'Lavender and lace maybe, but no corset. There are easier ways a resourceful old lady can pull herself together.'

'I'm married to the most resourceful woman I've ever known,' he complimented her.

'Hold to that thought,' she urged. 'You've already learned I can protect myself if needs be. You'll be playing your own dangerous game, Rick Braddock, and you'll have to keep your wits about you. We made an agreement when we got into the detective business, remember?'

'Right,' he nodded. 'When working undercover, we can't afford distraction, can't worry about each other's welfare. You're confident I can take care of myself and I have to be just as confident about you. And you know I am, honey. How could I ever forget Putnam, Nebraska?'

'Ah, memories,' she chuckled.

'The Ace High Saloon,' he recalled. 'We were still single. I was cleaning up at a poker party, you earning an honest buck singing to the customers – until that cattleman started mauling you. I even remember his name. Haley, Sid Haley. There I was, about to rush to your rescue ...'

'My hero.'

'... when you put him down, flat on his back. What a punch! A straight right to the jaw. The way you clobbered him was nothing short of magnificent. You want the truth, Hattie? It wasn't your beautiful face or your great legs – I remember the gown the management supplied had a slit skirt ...'

'You'd be bound to remember *that*.'

'A good investigator needs an eye for detail. It wasn't your tuneful singing either, nor the way your hair was swept atop your head. No. It was that beautifully timed punch. That's what did it for me, sweetheart. Then and there, I realised I was in love.'

'A sentimental sleuth,' she smiled. 'I warmly approve. But ...' She raised a finger warningly, 'never forget I'm the only woman you can be sentimental about.'

'You should fret,' he grinned. 'My roving eye stopped roving when first it focussed on my beloved Hattie.'

'Back to business,' she insisted while pouring their coffee. 'This afternoon you'll ...?'

'Book passage on tomorrow's southbound stage in the name of J. Fairchild, Esquire,' he said. 'And on the next day's southbound for Mrs E. Tebbut. Then I'm back here and reading all those notes you took during our parley with Mayor Leeson.'

'Five pages,' she offered. 'I've never written at such speed before. Everything he told us, it's all there. So you'll read it and – do some thinking?'

'A lot of thinking,' he frowned. 'Some planning too, maybe. It's all right for us to be light-hearted, honey, but let's not delude ourselves. This'll be quite a case. So many ramifications. I keep remembering the missing Gatling gun, but there's more, isn't there? The raid on an isolated gold claim, mine workers getting out of hand, soldiers throwing their weight around and a good sheriff forced to take a back seat while a narcisstic cavalry officer ...'

'The community's Major problem,' quipped Hattie.

'... has delusions of grandeur,' he scowled. 'Runs roughshod over the local administration, plays the despot and sees the civilians as his subjects.'

'What with one thing or another, it seems there is much to be done,' she remarked.

'By us,' he said.

'We'll manage,' she said confidently.

'Oh, sure.' He shrugged and grinned. 'The Braddock way. Remember how it used to be when you were an understudy and had to go on in a hurry, play the lead at short notice, unsure of your lines?'

'As if I could ever forget,' she said. 'Trying to pick up cues, the desperate ad-libbing.'

After lunch, Rick strolled to the stagecoach depot and made their bookings. His two-day journey to Shayville would begin 8.30 of the following morning, Hattie's 2pm of the day after. During the afternoon, he arranged for his packed Saratoga trunk to be delivered to the depot.

When they sat down to an early breakfast, Hattie ran a critical eye over her heavily-disguised husband. Rick hadn't overdone the make-up and what little he had used was effective. The costume was right, she decided. Grey pants, a checkered vest, white shirt with black string tie, an alpaca coat and his armpit-holstered .38 well-camouflaged. The wig was ash-grey and collar-length, matching the droopy moustache and short beard. He had greyed his eyebrows and donned steel-rimmed spectacles, the lenses unmagnified.

'Dear child ...' He addressed her gently, his voice quavery, 'your cuisine leaves nothing to be desired.'

'It's as though some old uncle of mine dropped in for breakfast,' she observed.

'Good enough, huh?'

'You'll get by. I know you'll stay in character.'

'Oldsters are my specialty. I'll remember to develop a stoop, walk slowly, dodder a little.'

'I'll miss you, you ham. Well, for a while.'

'And I'll eagerly await the arrival of Mrs Elmira Tebbut after I'm settled at Shayville. You know, kid, you could get lucky. Old Julius might take a shine to Mrs Tebbut and make a big play for her.'

'You're an incurable romantic, Rick Braddock.'

'Certainly am. But you – or any characters you impersonate – are the only women for me.'

'I should hope.'

The farewell was typical Braddock style. Shayville could be dangerous for one or both of them. This they well realised but, as was their way, they scorned all the old bromides. Rick did *not* remind Hattie how precious to him she was nor warn her to tread wary in

Shayville. And Hattie would not have been Hattie had she embraced him emotionally and begged him to be careful, shed a tear and reminded him he was all the husband she had. He already knew that.

'Showtime again,' he said as they kissed.

'Break a leg,' she chuckled.

En route to the stage depot, toting his valise, Rick moved along unhurriedly and stoop-shouldered, affecting the gait of a man who had celebrated his fiftieth birthday, and not too recently.

Another expediter was on duty this morning and the depot manager barely noticed the elderly gent boarding the southbound, so no eyebrows were raised. The guard secured Rick's grip on the roof with the other baggage, which included his trunk. The coach rolled out of Denver on schedule, passengers trading nods, the males touching their hatbrims to the two bombazine-gowned lady travellers.

Rick was given ample opportunity to practise his elderly gent voice. The scrawny, dapper man seated beside him, engaged him in conversation.

'Where're you headed, friend?'

'My destination, sir, is Shayville,' he replied.

'Pitney's the name, Orville Pitney. Liquor salesman. I represent the Collins and Cordroy company. You?'

'Julius G. Fairchild.'

'And you're headed for Shayville?'

'That is my intention.'

'Too bad.'

'Pardon?'

'Being a gentleman and respectable, you won't like it there. Your first trip?'

'I have never before visited Shayville.'

'Well, better you than me is all I can say. I had

regular clients there. Oh, sure. Used to write plenty
business in Shayville, specially at the Glad Hand
Saloon. The owner, Arlo Coventry, him and me got
to be good buddies. But, since Shayville got to be no
place for a peace-loving drummer, I don't do the
town nowadays. Quick lunch at the cafe by the stage
depot, then back on the stage. That's as far as I'll
budge.'

'There has been a change?'

'Better believe it. Big change. Ever heard of martial
law?'

'The term is familiar to me, Mister Pitney.'

'That's what they got in Shayville now. And those
troopers? I got to tell you. The minehands from the
ridge're a mean bunch, but I swear those soldier
boys're no angels. No, sir. Last time I overnighted
there, I made a dumb mistake, took a short cut along
a side alley. And the hard cases that clobbered me and
lifted my wallet, they sure weren't civilians.'

'You were assailed and robbed by soldiers?'

'No use complaining to the sheriff. When a town's
under martial law, the big boss is the top army man,
and he's a galoot with a chip on his shoulder against
civilians, won't hold still for any criticism of his
troopers.'

From the drummer, Rick listened to the same tale of
woe unfolded by Ben Leeson, but with variations.
Pitney assured him the towns at which they would
overnight before reaching Shayville were safe enough
for travellers. But, in Shayville, 'Mr Fairchild' would
be at risk. Pitney was booked all the way to Miller's
Ford on the Purgatoire, an orderly cattle-town, a
better environment for a gent of Mr Fairchild's
calibre. What did he want in a hell-hole like Shayville
anyway?

'I may seek employment there.'

'You'd want to work in a place like that?'

'There may be opportunities for me.'

'Well, Mister Fairchild, do yourself a favour. Think of everything I've told you – and take care.'

'I will be cautious,' Rick promised.

As the drummer had assured him, no unseemly incidents at noon and overnight stops, nothing to distress the gentle and courtly Mr Fairchild. But he heard more talk of his ultimate destination in restaurants and hotel lobbies. Shayville's notoriety was spreading. That paleface-hating renegade, Bearcat Webster, was believed to be holed-up somewhere in the area. Street brawls were not infrequent in Shayville; it was rumoured there was undeclared war between the diggers from Shay Ridge and the troopers from Camp Kemp and townsfolk craving peace and mindful of their welfare lived in a state of constant tension.

Eleven o'clock of the morning he would end his journey, Rick peered through the coach windows, scanning the terrain east and west.

'Headquarters of the Third Cavalry far over there to the east,' he mused. 'And away to the west, that would have to be Shay Ridge. The county seat dead ahead. All right, Braddock, it's *all* ahead of you, one hell of a situation, a mess to be cleaned up and everything set to rights – for twenty-five a day plus expenses.'

The Braddocks had established their detective agency less than a year before. He was a wily, nimble witted adventurer and not old enough, nowhere near old enough, to be as jaded as some veteran Pinkertons, some big city police officers. That was what he and his resourceful wife had going for them. Zest. Cunning. Versatility.

Neither Leeson nor the liquor drummer had exaggerated. He sensed the tension in the air as the stage rolled into the bustling mine town.

# 2

# Looks can be Deceptive

As they disembarked, Orville Pitney shook Rick's hand, wished him well and followed other passengers into the nearest cafe. On the porch of the stage depot, Rick accepted his grip from the guard and addressed the depot boss, requesting directions to a suitable hotel.

'Best place for you would be the Kirkland House,' he was told.

'Vacancies there?'

'Bound to be.'

'Thank you. I believe I'll register at once.'

'You do that. I'll have your trunk sent over.'

On his way to the hotel, Rick gave the main street and the buildings lining it a careful once-over. In the lobby, he set his valise down and traded pleasantries with the desk clerk, who was eager to please.

'Ground floor rear suit you, Mister Fairchild? Easier on you, right? No stairs to climb?'

'Most considerate of you. A ground floor rear will be satisfactory.'

'How long'll you be with us?'

'A week perhaps. May I pay one week's rent in advance? Should I decide to prolong my stay, I will of course …'

'That'll be fine. Just sign your John Hancock right there and here's your key. Dining room's open.'

Rick paid with a fifty. The clerk made change, he found his room and let himself in and his trunk was carried in some ten minutes later. The dining room was a touch depressing, but the food digestible. He returned to his room after lunch, donned the planter's hat that went with his old man get-up and studied his reflection in the dresser mirror.

'You'll pass muster,' he assured himself. 'Time to look for work, so what'll it be? A saloon job I think.'

In a place like Shayville, any saloon would be a good place for picking up information, listening to gossip, getting a handle on the town and its various factions. He was not without experience, could tend bar or any gambling layout and had been a bouncer on more than one occasion, so why not a saloon?

He locked his room, returned his key at the reception desk and ventured forth and, a few minutes later, was reminded that Shayville was as unruly a place as its mayor had described it.

The two troopers jostled him as he passed a side alley, forced him into it and demanded cash. They were flushed, truculent and, judging from the odours assailing Rick's nose, non-members of any temperance society.

'Twenty, old timer,' one of them growled.

'You oughtn't begrudge soldiers protectin' this town the price of a bottle or two,' leered the other one.

'And don't get no fool notion of bellyachin' to Sheriff Strother, that useless no-account,' he was warned. 'We ain't robbin' you. We're just partakin' of your generosity, savvy?'

The 'old timer' protested he had only $15 on his

person.

'That'll do. Hand it over.'

A fine show of indignation.

'I think not, you young blackguards!'

'C'mon, you old jackass. Are we gonna have to do this the hard way?'

'I think not,' Rick repeated, just before discouraging them.

With agility belying his appearance, he swung a kick to a belly, causing the recipient to double over and wheeze frantically. The other trooper was close enough to get in the way of Rick's right elbow, which was jabbed into his ribs with merciless force. That one groaned in anguish and reeled to the south side of the alley.

Unhurriedly, Rick returned to Main Street to canvass the saloons. The sore and sorry soldiers were temporarily forgotten. He was now recalling the name of a saloon mentioned by the talkative Orville Pitney and noting it was only a short distance away. Reaching it, he paused before entering, his ears cocked to familiar sounds, the clink of bottlenecks against glasses, the giggles of percentage women, the roulette man droning his spiel, 'Place your bets, gents', the rumble of talk. What was missing? Music.

Moving in, he studied the bar-room and the staff and customers. There were townsmen present and quite a few soldiers. His gaze switched to an upright piano. The keyboard cover was down.

The pudgy, pomaded man keeping a worried eye on the soldiers just had to be the proprietor, he decided. And as jittery a saloonkeeper as he had ever seen. He did his stoop-shouldered slow walk past the games of chance to where Arlo Coventry stood and presented himself.

'Good afternoon, sir. Julius Fairchild, at your service. You are, I presume, the proprietor of this fine establishment?'

'Yeah. Name's Coventry. What do you mean — at my service?'

'Mister Coventry, I seek employment.'

'Looking for work, huh? Sorry. Got nothing for you.'

'I'm an expert bartender and can supervise any game of chance you care to name.'

'Got a barkeep and all the dealers I need.'

'I'm also a musician. Mister Coventry, the piano is unattended. Dare I hope you had to fire your last pianist?'

Coventry's face clouded over. He winced.

'I didn't fire Nick,' he sighed. 'Poor feller had to fire himself. Listen, it's a sad story. I don't want to talk about it and, believe me, you wouldn't want to play piano here.'

'But I'm prepared to begin immediately. I'm available.'

'Forget it, old man. I'd be doing you no favour.'

Rick wheedled.

'Having aroused my curiosity, at least give me an explanation.'

Coventry gave in and explained, and Rick was at once intrigued. Small wonder the saloonkeeper was trying to forget the ugly incident, the brutality of a noncom of the 3rd Cavalry, Sergeant Gunther Hake, now quartered at what had once been Mayor Leeson's Grand Hotel. No music lover, the sergeant. Irritated by Nick's playing, he had ordered him to desist. Nick was half-way through a popular tune and went on playing until Hake strode to the piano and rammed the keyboard cover down on his fingers.

'The way Nick screamed – most terrible sound I've ever heard,' Coventry recalled, shuddering. 'Doc Albertson had to splint his busted fingers. Poor feller's in bad shape now. Somebody has to feed him and, when he needs to – you know what I mean – it's embarrassing for him.'

'A sad tale indeed,' said Rick. 'But I still require employment and am willing to take my chances.'

'It's not worth the risk!' protested Coventry.

'At least audition me,' begged Rick. 'See here, my fretful friend, I extend to you a fair offer, gentleman to gentleman. I will perform at no cost to you. Give me three hours at that instrument and if, at the end of that time, you decide against adding me to your staff, you'll owe me not a cent.'

'Well …' Coventry shrugged nervously. 'Be it on your own head – I mean your hands.'

Rick doffed his hat to the percenters, hung it up, shuffled to the piano, removed his coat and draped it over the chairback, seated himself and raised the cover. He vamped an intro and began playing the first bars of *The Sweetheart of Dan McGee*, a ballad well known to the patrons, also to Coventry's hired girls, all three of them, who gathered by the piano, linked arms and began singing the lyrics. They were off key, all three of them, but Rick beamed paternally at them.

When the song ended, there was desultory applause. Still beaming at the painted bawds, Rick mumbled,

'Ah, my dears, were I thirty years younger. Alas, age has its disadvantages.'

'Hey, don't quit hopin', Pop,' leered an overweight redhead. 'Might be life in the old dog yet.'

The women returned to coaxing customers to the

games of chance. Troopers came and went during the
next ninety minutes and, while playing piano, 'old
Julius' noted the behaviour of Major Royle's minions,
keeping his reaction to himself. Any of them wanting
to take the load off his feet tended to bully a
townsman into surrendering his chair, and the
townsmen rarely protested, didn't dare, he supposed.
Plainly, the citizens of Shayville had just cause for
their resentment of martial law and, just as plainly,
the soldiers considered themselves superior to mere
civilians.

He was still providing background music, playing a
Chopin piece he knew by heart, when the tall and
burly sergeant came swaggering in with a couple of
troopers in tow. A woman moved past Rick's chair,
not pausing, but softly warning.

'Watch yourself, Pop. That's Hake just came in.'

Welcomed by other troopers, Hake announced
he'd buy a round and bellowed to the barkeep to give
table service. Studying him without appearing to do
so, Rick took note of his brawn, his heavy features, his
bumptious demeanour; he gave special attention to
the big man's midriff, noting the bulge above the belt
knuckle. He continued to perform, seeming completely immersed in Chopin.

And then, after downing a shot of whiskey,
Gunther Hake glared over his shoulder at Rick and
reprimanded a jittery Arlo Coventry.

'Hey you! Warned you about that damn tinklin',
didn't I?'

Coventry signalled frantically. Rick played on,
pretending he hadn't noticed. In fury, Hake got to his
feet, reminded everybody he was no music lover and
advanced threateningly toward the piano.

'Professor, you better …' began the barkeep.

'Let up on that tinklin', you old goat!' ordered Hake. 'It gets on my nerves!'

'This is Chopin,' quavered Rick. 'It is meant to tinkle.' His fingers fluttered expertly over the keys. 'Excuse me. I must concentrate. This is an intricate piece.'

'I said stop!' growled Hake, moving closer.

Rick played on, nobody guessing he was ready for the big sergeant's next move. A cruel grin creased Hake's unappealing visage. Now he was close enough to reach a hand to the keyboard cover. He swung it down hard and fast and, forewarned, Rick drew his hands back with only moments to spare. A calculated risk; his fingertips were clear, but by just an inch.

'The last damn fool wasn't so lucky,' grinned Hake.

Rick went into his act, rising, moving around the piano to confront Hake, trembling in outraged indignation.

'You are a rogue and a fiend and a sadist!' he croaked. 'My hands could have been broken …!'

'That was the idea,' retorted Hake.

'You are a disgrace to the army!' accused Rick. This started Hake and the troopers laughing derisively. He gave them greater cause for mirth by dancing a jig of rage and bunching his fists. 'I'll not tolerate such blackguardly behaviour! I demand satisfaction! Prepare to defend yourself!'

More laughter. Hake guffawed, stood arms akimbo and called to his cohorts.

'How about this? Dumb old bastard wants to fight me!'

'Here it comes, sucker,' Rick was thinking.

The bulge about Hake's buckle was irresistible. He stepped forward, throwing everything behind a left to that target, remembering to pant as a man of advanced years over-exerting himself would surely do. The effect was devastating. Hake's hands hung at his sides, his complexion changing from florid to pasty grey. Startling his audience, Rick next swung his right fist over his shoulder baseball pitcher style, and with formidable force. Again he was on target. Hake's nose was suddenly bloody and his eyes glazed. He didn't crumple. He stood stiffly a moment before keeling over backward like a felled pine, and the crash as he hit the floor seemed to cause the glassware back of the bar to vibrate. He was down, and well and truly unconscious.

In the shocked silence that followed, Rick unclenched his fists and worriedly studied his hands.

'That was so *rash* of me!' he fretted. 'I may have damaged finger bones! I must test them at once!'

He reseated himself at the piano, raised the keyboard cover and, off the cuff, improvised and chanted a two-line jingle in a cracked tenor.

'Be upright kind sir, I implore,
You're a sorry sight, there on the floor.'

Then, peering over the piano top, he observed,

'Gad! He refuses to rise.'

That broke the tension. Locals and staff burst into laughter while the troopers gaped incredulously.

'I'm still trying to believe it.' Coventry couldn't help grinning. 'A man so old – cooling a soldier so big and tough.'

No longer intimidated, the barkeep pointedly remarked,

'Might be these soldier-boys ain't as tough as they'd like us to think.'

Thus encouraged, the saloonkeeper addressed the bug-eyed troopers.

'You'd better carry the sergeant out of here. It

doesn't look dignified, does it, a noncom just lying there, customers having to step over him? I don't think the major'd approve.'

The soldiers were slowly rallying from their shock. Some of them aimed uncertain glances at Rick as they struggled to lift Hake. Deputy Sheriff Roy Bass, barrel-chested and snub-nosed, was entering just as they began toting Hake from the bar-room. He stood aside to make way for them, frowning perplexedly.

With no more cavalrymen in the place, the deputy appealed to the grinning staff and locals.

'Please tell me Hake was clobbered by one of his own – not by a citizen.' He was eagerly informed that the sergeant had indeed been knocked senseless by 'the old feller at the piano'. Bemused, he stared across at Rick. 'That can't be. *He* cooled Hake? He wouldn't have the strength!'

'I am sick with shame.' Rick waxed contrite and rose shakily. 'I gave in to temper, did not realize what I was doing and – and now I feel faint.'

'Brandy for Julius,' Coventry ordered the barkeep. 'On the house.'

'No, no,' sighed Rick, raising a hand, making sure it trembled. 'But I feel – I should rest. If you'll permit, Arlo my friend, I'll rest in my room. By evening, I'll feel better. Be assured I'll return and ...'

'When you feel strong enough, Julius,' nodded Coventry. 'No hurry.'

After donning coat and hat, Rick apologized to the confused deputy and left to return to the Kirkland House. He walked there slowly, but with his brain working fast. Ideal time for a visit to the arrogant Major Royle, he decided. Ben Leeson's assessment of the man was accurate, he had no doubt, but know thy enemy, size him up personally, this militarist bighead so contemptuous of civilians.

He collected his key, let himself into his room, locked the door, lowered the windowshade and opened his trunk. One disguise was replaced by another in double-quick time; on the road with a repertory group, an enthusiastic actor learned to switch roles fast.

Julius Fairchild's wig, facial hair, etc, were replaced by the light brown hair, matching eyebrows and moustache of a man twenty years younger. The spectacles were discarded. Rick changed to a hound's tooth checked suit the pants of which were loose about the waist, permitting a little padding to make him appear paunchy. He donned a tan derby, checked through his supply of calling cards, chose and pocketed one and also equipped himself with notebook and pencil. He was as ready as he would ever be.

With the shade raised and the window open, he kept a wary eye on people, the few of them walking the back alley, until all backs were turned. He slipped out and walked two blocks uptown, affecting a jaunty strut. By way of a side alley, he moved into Main Street and on to the Grand Hotel.

Rifle-toting troopers stood either side of the main entrance, but not at attention, one of them smoking. He accorded them a cool nod as he climbed the steps and entered the lobby, there to be confronted by a corporal who demanded he state his business. Briskly, he produced the calling card.

'Oliver Hughes, feature writer, *Denver Chronicle*, here to interview your commanding officer. Show him the card, son. I'm sure he'll see me.'

'Mulligan,' called the corporal.

The lobby had lost much of its grandeur, Rick

covertly observed. How fortunate Mayor Leeson couldn't see it right now, the reception desk knife-scarred, the fine carpet showing dark patches into which cigar stubs had been ground, off-duty troopers lounging about.

Trooper Mulligan came to the fore.

'Take this gent up to the major's quarters,' instructed the corporal, returning Rick's card. 'The major'll want to see him. He'll always talk to news-papermen.'

As they climbed the stairs, the trooper remarked to Rick,

'Bridal suite.'

'Bridal suite?' Rick repeated in a nasal twang. 'So Major Royle's honeymooning here?'

'Nope,' grunted Mulligan. 'Bridal suite's the best in the place. Nothin' but the best for the major.'

'Ah,' nodded Rick. 'An officer with style. I like that.'

In the top floor corridor, they approached a half-open door. Mulligan paused and flinched. One of the voices audible from within was raised in anger. He gestured to a seat.

'Better wait there, mister. When Corporal Haley comes out, you can go right in.'

He disappeared, leaving Rick to seat himself and eavesdrop. The loudest voice he assumed to be Royle's, clipped speech, the authoritative tone accentuated.

'One enlisted man laid up with a cracked rib, another with severe abdominal pain – and now you tell me Sergeant Hake's nose has been broken – by a man old enough to be his father? Corporal Haley, this is preposterous!'

'Only reportin' what I heard, Major. I don't under-stand it, but that's how I heard it.'

'What in thunderation's happening to the Third? Confound those miserable civilians! Any of them who dares raise his hand to a soldier under my command will wish he'd never been born! Dismissed!'

'Sir!'

Corporal Haley emerged and would have passed the seated man had the seated man not held out a hand, presenting a card.

'Mind taking this to the major?'

Haley took the card, glanced at it, re-entered the room and, a few moments later, came out again and jerked a thumb.

'Major'll see you now.'

Rick moved into the room that had become the office of Company B's commanding officer, removed his derby and closed the door behind him. In one quick appraisal, he saw Royle to be exactly as he'd visualized him, an erect, square-shouldered six-footer of extreme military bearing, full dress uniform for pity's sake, buttons gleaming as brightly as the dark pomaded hair and the lovingly tended, waxed moustache. Good features. An undoubtedly hand-some man carrying a double load of conceit.

'Major Calvin Cornelius Royle, Third Regiment, United States Cavalry,' he beamed. He offered his hand, the gesture indicating his visitor should quiver with delight. 'A pleasure, Mister Hughes, always a pleasure to meet a gentleman of the press.' Glancing beyond Rick to the closed door, he frowned and asked, 'You're alone?' Rick nodded as they shook hands. Royle's grip was hard, a real flesh-bruiser, so he treated him to a little extra pressure; Royle was first to let go, 'No photographer?'

'Well, no, Major Royle.'

'I assumed you'd require a picture of me.'

'My editor's bound to insist, yes sir, Major. There'll be a *Chronicle* photographer headed for Shayville within an hour of Editor Dinsdale reading my copy. Barney Dinsdale likes my stuff. I do great interviews, greater articles.'

'Be seated, Mister Hughes. I'm busy – always busy – but I can spare you a little time. Questions?'

'Quite a few, sir.' Rick produced notebook and pencil. 'That Webster jasper, the half-breed Arapaho who led the massacre at the Lucky Seven claim. Webster is the prime suspect?'

'Webster's dirty work. As dangerous a renegade as ever there was. But, of course, he'll not stay free much longer. I'm determined to bring him to justice. And be it known, Mister Hughes, that any enemy running foul of me is on borrowed time.'

'I'll write that down as a direct quote. Stirring stuff, Major. Our readers'll be – well – there's only one word. Enthralled.'

'Naturally,' Royle agreed with a smug smile.

'Cunning adversary just the same, this Bearcat Webster,' suggested Rick. 'I mean – hijacking a Gatling gun right out of the Camp Kemp armoury ...'

'Impossible,' growled Royle. 'Webster wouldn't dare. I'm convinced treacherous whites of this region were responsible for that theft and the murders of the quartermaster sergeant and a trooper.'

'How about tracks?'

'The prints of moccasined feet, yes, a clever ruse.' The major grimaced distastefully. 'But moccasins worn by white civilians, Mister Hughes. The Gatling was stolen by locals. I deduced that immediately of course. And, believe me, the Gatling will be retrieved and the guilty parties punished. I suspect the Gatling is concealed in this town. It will be found, mark my words. My strategy will succeed.'

'And – uh – the strategy?'

'Regular searches – without notice – of every house in Shayville, every place of business. At this moment, the inhabitants of this miserable town are in fear of me, anticipating the inevitable.'

'So, just a matter of time?'

'I'm in command of Shayville and the men under my command are well disciplined. Crack troops, Mister Hughes. Yes, it's just a matter of time. B Company men will recover the Gatling. I don't expect it'll take longer than another week, two at most.'

'Yes sir, Major. Now what's your theory about the motive? Why would Shayville men commit such a heavy crime against the army?'

Royle raised his eyebrows.

'Isn't it obvious?' he challenged. 'They're trying to make me appear inept. Spite, Mister Hughes. Jealousy. They're jealous of my reputation as the most brilliant strategist of Colonel Cobcroft's command. Spiteful rogues will go to any lengths to discredit their betters.'

'That *is* the obvious motive,' Rick warmly agreed, somehow restraining himself from laughing in Royle's face. 'I'm ashamed it didn't occur to me rightaway.'

The interview lasted some ten more minutes. He took notes, playing his role of profoundly impressed newsman for all it was worth, much to the major's gratification. Before leaving, he announced he would be returning to Denver on the next northbound stage. Major Royle was humbly thanked for having granted a member of the Fourth Estate so much of his valuable time.

Back in his hotel room, rigging the changes again, Rick worked slowly and did some deep thinking.

While Oliver Hughes became Julius Fairchild again, he arrived at a conclusion. The Shayville situation was even worse than Mayor Leeson realized. Why in the name of sweet sanity had the commanding officer of the 3rd Cavalry assigned a bonehead like Royle to administer martial law here? The man was incredibly self-centred. His conceit knew no bounds. He had genius, oh yes, a genius for muddled thinking and the devising of wild theories. The Gatling purloined by Shayville citizens?

'If that's true,' he reflected, 'my name is Ulysses S. Grant, Junior.'

His own theory was forming now. Only one way Shayville people could be released from bondage of martial law. Somebody had to prove the army wasn't needed here, had *never* been needed here. And that somebody had accepted a retainer, was on the case and had better get results.

When, after an early supper, he returned to the Glad Hand in his Julius Fairchild get-up, he was deciding Sheriff Strother should be the next party with whom he compared notes. Ben Leeson had assured him Strother and his deputies were down-to-earth incorruptible lawmen dedicated to their work until shouldered aside by B Company of the 3rd Cavalry. So be it. He had no option but to accept Leeson's endorsement of the local badge-toters and join forces with them.

There were no ugly incidents at the Glad Hand this night, while the venerable old gent at the piano played to the clientele. Locals came by to drink at the bar or risk a few dollars at the games of chance, but troopers were giving the place a wide berth.

'I wouldn't have it any other way, Julius,' Coventry confided while Rick was taking a break. 'It's not true that one man's money's as good as another's. Give me a choice, my only customers'd be the old gang I've known for years, townsmen, my regulars. Those roughneck soldiers – who needs 'em?'

'Arlo, my good friend,' sighed Rick. 'I feel I owe you an abject apology.'

'For what?'

'My conduct this afternoon, my foolish reaction to the treatment I almost suffered at the hands of that ruffianly sergeant.'

'Foolish, you call it?'

'I'd never forgive myself if you were subjected to some form of reprisal. I'd hold myself responsible.'

'Forget it, old timer. You sure don't owe me any beg pardons. By damn, if a gent your age could knock Hake right off of his feet – which the whole town's talking about – it might be there'll be more than a few townsmen, young or old, who'll start hitting back at Royle's Roughnecks the way they sure as hell deserve.'

'It is all …' Rick heaved another sigh, 'most regrettable.'

'Only one thing I don't understand,' frowned Coventry. 'No offence, Julius, but you're no spring chicken. So how'd you suddenly get strong enough to clobber Hake so *hard* – and *twice*?'

'Passion, my friend,' said Rick. 'I was outraged and let my emotions get the better of me, which is unforgiveable.' He added a bare-faced lie. 'My muscles still ache from the effort.'

'I can see you're shaken by the whole thing,' Coventry said sympathetically.

'Severely,' nodded Rick.

'So I guess you won't be staying long,' said Coventry. 'A fine old music man like you, a gentleman, in a town as rough as this. That's okay, Julius. For as long as you want to hang around, you got a job here. And, when you decide you have to move on, that's okay too.'

'I appreciate that,' said Rick.

The sheriff's other deputy loafed in a short time later, treated himself to a beer and brought it to the piano to stare curiously at Rick. Billy Grimble was of similar physique to Roy Bass, barrel-chested, husky-looking. They did differ in the nasal equipment department; his nose was bulbous.

He identified himself, downed a mouthful of beer and asked in a wondering way,

'You're the one, huh? It was you punched the wind out of the big sergeant and busted his snoot?'

'It saddens me to confess I'm guilty of that act of violence, Deputy Grimble,' nodded Rick.

'You're too old to lay one on a galoot as big as Hake and make it count,' decided Grimble. 'So there was a trick to it. You gave yourself an edge, right? C'mon, old feller, 'fess up. You can tell me. It'll be our secret. Give you my word I'll keep it under my hat.'

'Pardon?' said Rick, strumming a few bars of *Maid of My Dreams*.

'You didn't use knuckle-dusters,' opined Grimble. 'Somebody would've noticed for sure. So what else? Roll of coins in each fist? Or maybe you keep a couple rocks in your pockets – just big enough to wrap your hands around. That'll do it every time.'

'No such devices, I assure you,' said Rick. 'I was, for a few terrifying moments, out of control. I completely lost my temper.'

'I'll be dogged.' The deputy shook his head. 'Well, okay, if you say so. But do me a favour. Don't ever get that mad at me.'

'That's most unlikely,' smiled Rick.

'Rather be your friend than cross you, you know?' grinned Grimble.

'There is no danger we'd ever become enemies,' Rick assured him.

After the deputy finished his beer and departed, a leading citizen well-known to Rick arrived. Mayor Ben Leeson was accorded an amiable welcome by Coventry. At the bar, he ordered and paid for a short shot of rye and drank it slowly. It was a little late for a tune as lively as *Turkey in the Straw*, but Rick was pounding it out with gusto. The mayor propped an elbow on the bar, drummed his fingers in time with the beat for a while, then gazed across at the performer. Like Coventry and both deputies, he too was intrigued. Fortunately, when he moved across to confer with the piano player, no other patrons were in earshot.

'Leeson's the name,' he offered, while Rick played on. 'Ben Leeson. I'm mayor of this town.'

'Julius Fairchild, sir,' quavered Rick. 'I am honoured to meet so distinguished a gentleman.'

'I can't say I've been feeling distinguished lately,' grouched Leeson. 'Don't even feel like I'm mayor any more. Listen, friend, I'm curious. They tell me you beat hell out of that noncom with all the muscle, Gunther Hake, and that's kind of hard to believe.'

'No shock reaction, if you please,' Rick begged in his old man's voice. 'And do not raise your voice.' Then, in the voice Leeson remembered, 'He was a pushover, Boss. Wide open for a left to the belly and a right to the face.'

Leeson's eyes bulged; he grasped at the top of the piano for support.

'Holy Moses!' he breathed.

'Not even close.' Rick grinned and winked. 'Just me, half of the Braddock Agency on the job. Better go home now and get your sleep. Pleasant dreams, Mayor Leeson.'

The Mayor went home in a daze.

At midnight, the Glad Hand closed for the day and Rick returned to his hotel room. And, as he prepared to retire, he began thinking of his beautiful – also audacious – wife.

# 3
# Scouting Expedition

How would Hattie begin? he wondered. Quietly maybe, after sizing up the Shayville scene. Or, just as likely, in a spectacular way. With Hattie, it didn't pay to attempt predictions. She was her own woman, imaginative, wily, independent and, in a crisis, quick-thinking. Rick adhered to all the traditional protective instincts where his wife was concerned, but acknowledged she could make it on her own. He could afford to concentrate on his own chores, leaving her a free hand.

He thought, before lapsing into slumber, of the look of Main Street during his walk from the Glad Hand to the hotel, the many minehands and troopers still hanging about. Rough men and unruly. Shayville was a powderkeg with a short fuse. That fuse had to be cut before some fool touched it off. His task, his assignment, his and Hattie's. And, as always, they would have to improvise.

'One step at a time,' he decided. 'Establish friendly relationships with the local law first thing in the morning and move on from there.'

Sufficient unto the day. He slept.

Since the imposition of martial law, not much

action at the county jail fronted by the sheriff's office. When, at 9am, Sheriff Vin Strother arrived to rouse Curly Middlecott, the live-in jailer, he was in sour mood. Curly no longer unlocked cells to release troublesome drunks installed overnight. The ageing turnkey was becoming lazy, business being slack nowadays. With the army in control, Strother and his deputies had to defer to Royle. Troopers, not civilian lawmen, now kept roughneck miners in line. Or went through the motions.

This morning, a break in the monotony. Climbing the steps to the law office porch, Strother appraised the elderly gent seated in a caneback by the locked door. He at once identified the stranger; both deputies had stopped by his home to describe the piano-player who put sadistic Sergeant Hake down, flat on his back on the floor of the Glad Hand bar-room.

Rick used his old man voice, but dropped it an octave or two.

'Sheriff Strother?' he asked, rising and offering his hand.

'And you'll be Fairchild, him that busted the snoot of Gunther Hake,' Strother frowned as they shook hands. 'Got to say I'm mighty impressed, Mister Fairchild, mighty curious too.'

'If you allow me a few minutes of your valuable time,' Rick requested while Strother unlocked and opened the door.

'Huh!' grunted Strother. 'Since Major Royle took over, I got *too much* free time.'

He ushered Rick into a quite spacious office well-furnished. Two desks, a file cabinet, ample chairs, a stove, a well-stocked gunrack, a couch and, to the right of the jailhouse door, a wallmap of Shay

County and surroundings. The jailer rose from the couch knuckling sleep from his eyes, a wizened old timer, his surviving hair snow-white and nestling above and around his ears. He made straight for the stove to brew coffee, while Strother hung up his hat, revealing that, as well as being of scrawny physique, not an ounce of excess fat about his midriff, he had retained his iron-grey thatch.

'Before we get to what you want to talk about,' he said, seating himself at his desk and gesturing his visitor to a chair, 'you're gonna have to explain something to me. I still can't make sense of it, Mister Fairchild, you beating hell out of a man Hake's size and weight.'

'I'm Julius Charles Fairchild, Sheriff,' said Rick. 'When I'm with friends, men I can trust, I answer to Chuck. May I call you Vin? And may I speak in confidence? What I have to tell you, and everything else we discuss, had better be a tight secret. That's absolutely imperative.'

'Fine by me, Chuck,' offered Strother. 'You can speak free with Curly here. He's a clam.'

'Never was no blabbermouth,' Curly mumbled.

'And that goes for my deputies,' declared Strother. 'So come on now, Chuck, what's your secret? How do you *do* a thing like that?'

'Age need not affect the reflexes nor the muscle power,' Rick confided. 'Sioux medicine men understand about the maintenance of the body's strength. It was from them I learned the system. I used to be an army scout, lived with the Sioux for a while, other tribes too. It's – uh – kind of technical, Vin. Self-hypnosis is part of it. Once you've perfected the system, you just use it when the need arises. Look, it would take hours to explain it all, days, weeks. So you'll just have to accept my word.'

'I'll be dogged.' Strother was profoundly impressed.

'How come you palaver so all-fired educated?' frowned Curly.

'Self-education, Curly,' shrugged Rick. 'I support myself nowadays in many ways. I've even been a schoolteacher. Right now, I'm content to earn an honest dollar as a saloon piano-player.' He waxed reminiscent. 'Not like the old days, the hunting and trapping, the exploring. I knew them all, you know. Jim Bridger …'

'You knew Jim Bridger?' Curly asked incredulously.

'Long time back,' said Rick. 'I was just a kid then.'

'How about Bill Cody?' prodded Strother.

'Good man, Bill,' Rick acknowledged. 'Haven't downed a shot of whiskey with him in many a year. Last I heard, he was thinking of getting into the show business. I'm not sure that Buntline feller's a good influence on him.'

'Well, maybe I savvy it better now,' said Strother. 'You clobbering Hake. So what'd you want to talk to me about?'

'Vin, martial law can be a blessing to honest townsfolk,' opined Rick. 'But that's not how it's working in your bailiwick, is it? You have an intolerable situation here.'

'As if you need to remind me,' grouched Strother.

'Only one way out of it, my friend,' declared Rick. 'Only one way martial law will be revoked and the cavalry recalled to Camp Kemp. You have to prove they aren't needed here.'

'Tall order,' argued Strother.

'Can be done.'

'Tell me how.'

'Simple. You accomplished something big. You succeed where the major has so far failed.'

'You want to make that clearer?'

'Well, consider this. Supposing you pulled off something special. For instance, you, your deputies and a few reliable locals sprung a trap on Bearcat Webster, and drew his teeth once and for all? Or let's suppose you recovered that hijacked Gatling and returned it personally to the C.O. of the Third Cavalry? That'd make you a smarter man than Royle could ever hope to be. Colonel Cobcroft would have to admit it and you'd be justified in assuring the state administration you don't need help from the army in Shayville, you're all the law Shayville needs.'

Strother exhaled noisily.

'Great – just wonderful – but a pipe-dream.'

'Maybe not, if I lend a hand,' said Rick, rising and moving to the wallmap. 'Show me, Vin, and talk to me. Tell me everything, all the known facts of how that Gatling was stolen away from the Camp Kemp armoury.'

'You honestly think you could …?' began Strother.

'I make no promises,' said Rick. 'But let's not forget I used to be a scout.'

Strother joined him. They drank coffee offered them by Curly – not the best Rick had ever tasted – while the boss-lawman pointed to areas of importance, the location of the regimental headquarters at Camp Kemp to the north, the open terrain, a great deal of it, between Camp Kemp and, far to the south, the Laberinto Hills, believed to be Bearcat Webster's hideaway.

'How many sets of footprints found? – jog my memory, Vin.'

'Three. Moccasin prints. Well, three Arapahos'd be strong enough. They could easily have toted the Gatling and the ammunition away after they butchered the quartermaster noncom and the soldier.'

'Pursuit party, of course.'

'Sure. But the troopers tagged the tracks only a little way south that morning. Big wind blew up, swept all tracks away, so they had to turn back. My hunch is the Arapahos had horses waiting farther south, maybe a travois. That's how they hauled the gun to Bearcat's secret camp.' Strother returned to his chair. 'Meantime, that jackass Royle's got the fool notion ...'

'Shayville men committed that atrocity, disguised as Indians,' nodded Rick, still studying the map. 'Ridiculous, but typical of him. Tell me, Vin, if I rented a horse right now and rode out to those flats for a little scouting, could I be back in town by noon?'

'On a good horse maybe,' nodded Strother. 'If not noon, one o'clock or thereabouts. That's what you're gonna do?'

'It may help,' said Rick. 'Who knows? Always the chance I'll pick up a clue, or at least get a useful idea or two.'

'Devoy's Barn,' advised Curly. 'If he ain't rented it out, ask for the dapple geldin'. He's got a name – Abraham. Helluva good horse.'

'I'm obliged to you, Curly,' Rick said as he began leaving. 'Remember now, gentlemen. Secrecy.'

'Count on it,' said Strother. 'All the luck, Chuck.'

While seeking the Devoy barn, Rick sighted Hake a block away and gave thanks Hake hadn't seen him. He had no time to waste on a brutish cavalryman. The sergeant looked a mite the worse for wear, adhesive plaster showing stark on the region between eyes and mouth.

The dapple was available. A stablehand saddled it for him and then he was on his way, riding east from Shayville to explore the probable route followed by the Gatling hijackers. With the town well behind him, he heeled the dapple to a run; the animal responded well and, soon, he was travelling the area he had memorized while reading the sheriff's map. Wide open country, he observed. A vast plain. Neither the army camp nor the hills to the south visible.

'Lonely terrain,' he reflected.

Only two outstanding features that he could see. Ahead, a semi-circle of tall rocks. Some forty yards east of those boulders, a stand of trees. Automatically, he made for the rocks. Nature called. He could have reined up anywhere on the flats to relieve himself, but gentlemanly instincts die hard; he just naturally rode to the privacy of the rocks.

Dismounting, he ground-reined the horse and moved afoot into the semi-circle and on to its far side. After urinating and rebuttoning his fly, he began returning to the dapple. He paused, frowning. The ground had felt hard underfoot when he followed the curve of the rocks. Now, crossing diagonally, he had felt his boots sinking into slightly softer earth.

For a few moments he stood there, eyes downcast. This, surely, was too much to expect. He had been lucky in the past, but this was freakish, bizarre. A significant find, so early in his investigation?

He moved forward two paces, then backward a few, then sidestepped to left and right. An oblong of ground was undoubtedly softer than the area surrounding it. Still incredulous, he dropped to his knees and dug in with his hands, scooping earth out.

It then occurred to him that, working this way, it could take him a long time to excavate the whole section. With a pickaxe and spade, he could work faster, could unearth what had been buried here – if indeed anything *had* been buried here. And what reward for his effort? He might well exhume the remains of some poor son of a gun interred privately by his cohorts. It didn't *have* to be the Gatling. And why would the hijackers bury it anyway?

Rick Braddock was always a realist, but never an atheist. He was moved to voice a few remarks to his Maker. Respectfully of course. He was on his knees, so this seemed an appropriate time for it; he thought to remove his hat before raising his eyes skyward.

'There is *no* luck. There is only what You decree,' he conceded. 'What can I say? If, in Your mysterious way – and I *do* mean mysterious – You've decided I should so easily locate that which was purloined from Camp Kent. I thank You in advance. If I find only bones – well – Thy will be done, and thanks just the same.'

He replaced the disturbed earth, leaving it just as he found it, got to his feet and returned to the dapple. Before starting back, he lit a cigar and gazed away to the north and south. The half-way mark, he was thinking, again conjuring up a mind picture of Strother's map. Yes, this could well be the half-way point between the headquarters of the 3rd Cavalry and the secret headquarters of Bearcat Webster somewhere within the Laberinto Hills.

He nudged his mount to movement, still cogitating.

Assuming Bearcat himself, with just two of his followers, had pulled off that audacious coup, why cache the gun? Why hadn't they continued on to the hills to the south? The wind-storm? Yes, that could be the reason. In poor visibility, even redmen could be apprehensive, fearing they would lose their way. So maybe it made some kind of sense that, upon reaching the rocks, they decided to bury the Gatling.

Next question. If this were so, was it still buried there? Strong possibility. Some little time had elapsed since the hijacking. If the Gatling were in Bearcat Webster's possession, would he not have used it by now? This half-breed was a fanatic, white men his sworn enemies.

While headed back to town, he decided it was too early to discuss his hunch with Vin Strother. Why build false hopes? Better to wait till he was absolutely sure. Late tonight, after the town closed down, he would return equipped with a pickaxe and spade. But not a lantern. Hell, no. Just hope for moonlight.

At noon, when the southbound stage arrived on schedule, Rick was still some distance east. When his mental processes were busy with theories and questions, he preferred to ride slowly, the better to concentrate.

Hattie's disguise was as effective as her husband's. She alighted in a travelling gown of simple design, the fit camouflaging her eye-catching figure. Her brows were greyed to match her wig. Her headgear was a bonnet, not too austere, but certainly not frivolous. Make-up hid the roses in her cheeks. In age, she appeared to be fifty or so. She was careful not to move briskly nor too gracefully when she stepped up to the sidewalk. While other passengers disembarked, she addressed the depot-boss, politely requesting the name of a quiet hotel.

Had she asked for Shayville's best hotel, the depot boss would still have recommended the Kirkland House. He always recommended the Kirkland House;

the proprietor was his brother-in-law.

'Your baggage, ma'am?'

'One valise, one trunk.'

'Fine. I'll have a porter load 'em on a pushcart. You follow him, and the people at the Kirkland'll take good care of you.'

'Thank you very much. People are so kind.'

Her voice was in character with her disguise; the depot-manager felt for her, so much so that he tried to prepare her.

'Hope you have a happy stay, happy and safe. Wish I could guarantee that, Miss Tebbutt, but I'd be lying if I called Shayville a peaceful town. A lot of mining hereabout, you see. The miners played too rough, so we're under martial law now. That'd be good for everybody, specially the respectable folks, but I got to warn you the soldiers're as rough as the miners – rougher even.'

'How distressing,' sighed Hattie. 'I do appreciate your warning, sir, and I assure you I'll be most careful.'

The porter unloaded her baggage. Following him to the Kirkland House, she warily scanned Main Street and the people out and about. Minehands not working the diggings at this time were very much in evidence and as ruffianly a bunch as she had ever seen. Very visible too were cavalrymen. As Mayor Leeson had complained, they were no better than hard cases in uniform.

In the lobby, she won a polite greeting from the desk clerk. She rewarded him with a gentle smile and paid some attention to the open register, immediately noticing an alias and a room number. As the clerk offered a pen, she said shyly,

'I'm not terribly superstitious, but six is supposed to be my lucky number. Is it available?'

'Well, yes, Mrs …?'

'Tebbutt.'

'It's a ground floor rear, yours if you want, Mrs Tebbutt. How long …'

'A week, I should think.'

'Certainly. Just sign the register, and welcome to the Kirkland House. I'll have the porter fetch your baggage. Here's your key, ma'am.'

For Hattie, the process of settling in began. Her baggage arrived. She unlocked the valise, not the trunk, and did some unpacking. From the window, she checked the back alley and mentally complimented her husband.

'Ready for anything, as usual. Trust you to choose a room you can leave and re-enter in secret.'

After making the most of the lunch served her in the hotel dining room, she sallied forth to familiarize herself with Shayville. She was a full three blocks away when Rick returned the dapple to the Devoy barn.

While paying the stablehand, he added a tip and requested that the dapple be available for him later.

'Sometime after midnight. Can't be sure of the exact time. If you're taking a nap, I won't disturb you.'

'Sure you can …?' began the stablehand.

'Despite my years, I can still manage to saddle a horse,' Rick assured him. 'But I thank you for your concern, friend. Such kindness warms my heart.'

On his way to the nearest hardware store, he was resolving to lunch at a cafe, Mexican if he could find one. Busy morning. He had an appetite for chili con carne.

The hardware merchant irritated him more than somewhat. He had nothing personal against beady eyes, thick lips and scruffy moustaches, but this character was overly familiar and, worse still, overly inquisitive.

'You want to buy a pickaxe and shovel?' he was challenged. 'Old feller like you? Hey, at your age, you'd never make it as a prospector.'

'Mr Fairchild,' quavered testily.

'Sir, I have no intention of becoming a prospector. Will you kindly supply me with a pickaxe and spade?'

'All right, old feller, keep your shirt on.' The merchant looked out the required items. 'Here you go.'

'The price?'

The merchant named his price. Rick paid him the exact amount and demanded his purchases be wrapped.

'You want 'em *wrapped*?'

'That is what I said, or do you have a hearing problem?'

'I'll wrap 'em if you want.'

'Then do so!'

Having wrapped the pickaxe and spade, the storekeeper was still curious.

'What do you want 'em for, if you aren't gonna stake a claim?' he demanded.

'For digging my own grave,' said Rick.

The merchant's eyebrows shot up.

'Nobody digs their own grave,' he protested.

'I presume you're familiar with an old saying?' challenged Rick. 'If you want a thing done properly …'

'But you aren't dying – are you?' blinked the merchant. 'You're old, but you don't look sickly to me.'

'On the contrary,' scowled Rick, gathering up his purchases, 'I am in dire danger of being bored to death by an inquisitive storekeeper!'

He left the hardware merchant in a bug-eyed,

sagging-jawed condition, trudged out of the store and back to the hotel to stow the tools in his room. A short time afterward, he was enjoying lunch at Hernando's, a Mexican cafe on a side street, and Hattie was perusing with interest a hand-printed notice tacked to the front wall of the Shayville Community Hall on North Main Street.

'Inaugural meeting,' she mused. 'First get-together of the LRC which, it says here, stands for Ladies Reform Committee. Chairlady, Chloe Leeson. Mayor Leeson's wife? Probably.'

Well, well, well. So the demoralized distaff side of the local citizenry were organizing. The meeting to begin at 8pm sharp. She would attend, she decided. Had to start somewhere, didn't she? A chance to size up local ladies of good repute who, according to Ben Leeson, had been fair game for ruffianly minehands and just as ruffianly troopers for far too long. Might it be that she could contribute to the cause, if only with a helpful suggestion or two?

Upon returning to the Kirkland House, she requested and was handed her key, and noted that the key to Room 8 still dangled from its numbered hook on the rack. Rick would be back sooner or later, she assured herself. He would remember her chosen alias, note she was in the room next to his and, if he felt the time was right, would visit her, or vice versa. Then, no doubt, they would compare their reactions to the Shayville scene.

Leaving Hernando's, Rick supposed he should report for duty at the Glad Hand. The southbound stage had come and gone, however, which meant Hattie was now in town. Which hotel? he wondered. Too much to hope she had checked into the Kirkland? Only one way to find out.

In the lobby, when the clerk turned to unhook his key, he stole a glance at the open register. Great. Not only was she here; she was in Room 6, right next door.

He entered the rear corridor and was pleased to observe it was deserted. Letting himself into his room, he crossed to the window and opened it. When he glanced out, locals walking the back alley paid him no attention. He paid attention to the window of Room 6. He removed his hat and thrust his head out.

'Pssstt!'

A grey-wigged female head minus bonnet was thrust out of the next window.

'Pssstt yourself.'

'Be right with you, honey.'

He withdrew, closed and secured the window, moved into the corridor and paused to rap gently at the door numbered 6.

'Who?' inquired the 'old lady' within.

'Julius Fairchild – in person. Good madam, I believe we're already acquainted. May I make so bold as to …?'

'Make bold, by all means, sir.'

Hattie opened the door. He entered, closed it behind him, grinned and spread his arms.

'Come here, Beautiful.'

'Coming,' she smiled. 'But we'll have to make do with a hug, darling. Our make-up. Your whiskers.'

'The things I do for the Braddock Detective Agency,' he remarked as they hugged.

She sat on the edge of the bed. He drew a chair close and straddled it.

'You've been here longest, so you first,' she urged. 'Any progress, or is it too early to ask?'

'Hattie, I've surprised myself.'

'You've done that before. So talk to me. Dear old Miss Tebbutt is seething with curiosity.'

He brought her up to date, his job at the saloon, his clash with the brutish Sergeant Hake, his interview with and assessment of Major Calvin Royle, his secret parley with Sheriff Strother, then ...

'You aren't gonna believe this next bit.'

'Why? Are you about to lie to me?'

'No. Gospel truth,' he declared. 'And it's possible I'm clutching at straws. Just the same, I have to dig deeper into what I found this morning.' He went on to describe his discovery of disturbed earth in isolated terrain and watched her reaction. 'Too far-fetched?'

'A piece of the Third Cavalry's armoury, hijacked and planted *there*?' she frowned. 'Why would the Indians ...?'

'I keep asking myself that same question and, sweetheart, I can't forget what I found. From the looks of it, the hole could be big enough to contain the Gatling. So I have to sneak out there again.'

'When?'

'After the saloon closes. The wee small hours.'

'And, if you do unearth that terrible weapon?'

'I'll have some more thinking to do – a *lot* of thinking. Your turn now. Anything so far?'

'I'll be attending a meeting tonight,' said Hattie. 'It seems Mayor Leeson's wife is in the process of forming an all-female organization, the LRC.'

'Could stand for Let's Run for Cover.'

'Ladies Reform Committee.'

'Uh huh. Might be the girls're getting desperate.'

'I hope they're desperate enough, Rick. Never underestimate the fair sex. And, who knows? I may be able to help. In any event, this will be an opportunity for me to assess the mettle of the local matrons. And spinsters, of course.'

'Can't do any harm.'

'Thanks for the vote of confidence. If I can rally those long-suffering victims of lecherous miners and soldiers, we could do plenty of harm – to men who deserve it. And it'll be one in the eye for the almighty Major Royle. Just between us, darling, is he as dedicated a blowhard as Ben Leeson told us, is he as pompous?'

'Pompouser.'

'There's no such word.'

'There ought to be. And it'd fit Royle like a tight glove. I've run into some egotists in my time but, believe me, Royle really *works* at it.'

Hattie smiled and winked.

'Aren't you curious?' she challenged. 'I spoke of rallying the local ladies.'

'All right, I'm curious,' he nodded. 'Just what kind of rallying do you have in mind? A deputation of fearsome females marching on the Grand Hotel carrying banners – right through the lobby and upstairs to the mayor's private quarters – nagging him out of his mind?'

'There are better ways of embarrassing him.'

'Such as?'

'Well, if I'm persuasive enough, if I can convince the girls of their right to defend themselves against marauding males of the species ...'

'Even showing them a trick or two?' grinned Rick.

'What do you think?' she asked. 'Am I being too ambitious? Tell me. I respect your opinions.'

'Come on now,' he chuckled. 'You don't need my opinion, my permission nor my encouragement. I've seen how you protect yourself against woman-maulers and, to put it mildly, you're good at it.' He

became serious. 'You're right anyway, honey. All
women are entitled to defend themselves. So
anything you can teach Mrs Leeson and her friends
can only do more harm than good to heavy-handed
miners – and Royle's Roughnecks. Go get 'em,
sweetheart. Give it your best shot.'

'Where to next?' she said as he got to his feet.

'They'll be expecting me at the Glad Hand,' he told
her.

'You know that's quite a disguise,' she observed.
'You really do look ages older, and so venerable.'

'If you age gracefully, and I'm sure you will, you
could end up looking pretty much as you look right
now,' he complimented her. 'The clothes would be
more stylish, of course, the coiffure more
becoming ...'

'Well, I should hope.'

'Take care, huh?'

'You too – dear Mister Fairchild.'

When Rick began performing at the Glad Hand,
troopers of the 3rd Cavalry were conspicuous by their
absence. Very much in evidence, however, were
off-duty minehands in town for some heavy drinking,
heavy gambling and heavy anything else they could
get away with.

It didn't surprise him that roughneck prospectors
demanded he play the tunes they preferred. *My
Darling Clementine* for instance. He obliged.

Toward sundown, Deputy Roy Bass drifted in,
bought a beer and positioned himself beside the
piano-player.

'Vin told me and Billy about your little parley,' he
quietly confided. 'Like you to know we're with you –
Chuck – hundred percent. Any plan you cook up,
you can count on us as sure as you can count on Vin.'

'Good to hear, Roy,' Rick replied just as quietly. 'But this isn't the place. When we get together, your boss's office is the place, the door locked, strict privacy.'

'Gotcha,' nodded Bass. 'Me and Billy just want you to know.'

'Much appreciated, Roy. Do *you* have a request, any tune you'd like me to play?'

'Has anybody writ a song called "The Army Gives Me A Pain"?'

'I don't believe so.'

'Too bad. Somebody oughta.'

At 7.45pm, the gentle Miss Tebbutt emerged from the Kirkland House and began a sedate walk uptown, her destination the Community Hall. And managed to walk a whole block before being accosted. The man was roughly garbed, obviously a miner. He blocked her way, looked her over and chuckled wheezily; she flinched from the impact of his booze and tobacco breath.

'You're no young'un,' he leered. 'But maybe not too old, huh?'

'I beg your pardon, sir,' she murmured, feigning apprehension.

'Not too old for it.' He leaned closer. 'You know what I mean. Sure you do. A little fun?'

'I have something for you,' she said, and delved into her reticule.

'We're doin' fine,' he approved. 'You never seen me before and, already, you got a present for me.'

'Now where *did* I put it?' she frowned. 'Ah, yes. Here it is.' He backstepped, blinking in astonishment at the Remington derringer gripped in her hand. 'Tell me, when you're at work, pounding at all that hard rock, which arm do you find is the strongest, your right or your left?'

'Uh – look – I ...'

'If you do not disappear – quickly – I'll shoot at both your arms. How then will you swing a pickaxe or use a spade?'

'Listen, I'm goin' – I'm goin'!'

'That would be very nice,' smiled Hattie.

The miner left her hastily. She continued on to the Community Hall, the derringer out of sight again.

# 4
# Ladies' Night

Slender, soberly-gowned and painfully self-conscious Chloe Leeson was somewhat less than a forceful speaker. Hattie, seated to the rear of this gathering, felt for her. Assembled were a cross-section of the female citizenry of Shayville, giving Madam Chairwoman their undivided attention.

'What can I tell you, dear friends of mine?' The mayor's wife gestured helplessly. 'These are difficult times for us, none of us, not even older ladies, spared the improper advances of unruly miners and slovenly soldiers now infesting our town. Sheriff Strother and his deputies, whom we all trust, are so restricted now. We have to do something, but I don't know what. So the chair is open to suggestions. But, please, ladies, one at a time.'

First on her feet, the oldest and tiniest woman present brandished a furled umbrella and ferociously insisted they should buy guns and shoot any man accosting them.

Another woman pointed out the obvious perils of such action. They were more accustomed to raising children, cooking meals and keeping house than using firearms. Innocent parties could suffer injury or worse, it being a known fact that, when a firearm is discharged, the bullet has to hit something – or somebody – if the woman using said firearm is lacking in experience.

The whole membership of the LRC became vocal, but in an indecisive way. Hattie took this as her cue, got to her feet and called to Chloe Leeson.

'I am a newcomer, but aware of your predicament and in complete sympathy, Madam Chairwoman. Do I have your permission to address the meeting? I believe my practical suggestions may be beneficial.'

'By all means,' nodded Chloe.

With all eyes on her, Hattie walked the centre aisle and ascended to the stage. She then bestowed a sweet smile on her audience and began her pitch.

'I am Mrs Elmira Tebbutt, a widow just arrived in your community. I am also a foundation member of the WSDL, The Womens' Self Defence League, established by my dear friend Miranda Hardnut of Denver. Mrs Hardnut has, for some years, collaborated with the law authorities of the capital of this great state. The League, good ladies of Shayville, is dedicated to the rights of women, specifically our right to protect ourselves, and I am here to form a local chapter and demonstrate survival techniques.'

Right after she delivered that preamble, the meeting was intruded upon. Three hefty minehands came trudging in, one of them toting a bottle, another loudly announcing they were in party mood. The local women showed a variety of reactions, apprehension, indignation, tension, pained resignation, etc. Chloe Leeson was aghast but, though these boozing intruders did not realize it, Hattie was delighted to see them.

The third intruder pointed to the old upright left of stage.

'Pianner up there,' he leered. 'How about one of you gals give us some music for dancin'? And we'll all get friendly – and I mean *real* friendly!'

'Leave at once,' Chloe ordered, but timidly.

Again, Hattie grabbed for her cue, an opportunity too opportune to pass up.

'Ladies, these fiends are typical of the riff raff against whom I am trained to defend myself!' she declared. One of the miners called her a killjoy, also an old sow, asserted *she* was leaving – *he'd* see to that – and approached the stage. 'Watch carefully, ladies!'

The man climbed to the stage.

'Mrs Tebbutt, how can a lady of your years hope to …?' began Chloe.

'By improvising – like so,' explained Hattie, as the hard case advanced on her.

He growled at her and grasped her left arm. Simultaneously, she swung the edge of her right hand with devastating accuracy straight to his Adam's apple. He promptly released her, his eyes bulging, and backstepped.

'I don't care how old she is!' scowled the second man. 'No damn female's gonna treat a buddy of mine that way!'

'Method Number Two,' Hattie announced as he bounded up to the stage.

When he was close enough, about to reach for her, she swung a kick to his groin. He retreated, ashen and wheezing. Chloe clasped a hand to her bosom. A woman in the front row loosed a shocked gasp as the third miner, determined to avenge the humiliation suffered by his compadres, vaulted onto the stage. He rushed Hattie, who stood her ground, still a model of matronly dignity, but with her right fist bunched. She straight-armed her would-be assailant, a hard one

right to the jaw, causing him to recoil with his mouth
bloody.

'One of the more conventional dissuaders,' she told
her gaping audience. 'Quite effective, as you can see.
Less predictable than slapping the molester's face,
which rarely discourages them anyway.'

'Hey, Mrs Tebbutt's got the right idea, girls!' A
woman of ample proportions lumbered to her feet and
appealed to her friends. 'Ella, Jane, Molly – what're we
waiting for?'

Moments later, four troopers swaggering past the
meeting hall were struck by a human missile and
knocked off balance. Before they could pick themselves up, four over-stimulated women gave the
second minehand the old heave ho, hurling him from
the front doorway. That one was deposited atop a
half-prone soldier; the third struck two soldiers temporarily upright.

The troopers took umbrage and began beating up
on the miners, who rallied and aimed blows at anything in a uniform, with the result that seven men were
now staging a pitched brawl in the middle of Main
Street.

Happening upon this scene of conflict, Deputy Billy
Grimble made to step off the east sidewalk and
intervene. Then he checked himself. What the hell?
With the town under martial law, he was no longer
authorised to break up such violent disturbances. So
he should worry?

'Let 'em get their lumps, let 'em get hurt bad. That'll
make seven less plug-uglies for us to fret about.'

He withdrew to a neutral vantage point, an alley-
mouth, rolled and lit a cigarette and contentedly
watched the combatants inflict and suffer pain.
Couldn't happen to a nicer bunch of fellers.

Hattie, now the heroine of the night, was being kept busy demonstrating "The Hardnut Methods" to admirers joining her on stage, the better to watch and memorize. The ladies were fascinated. As Hattie calmly explained, there were so many simple deterrents, so many options for women of respectable background desirous of repelling mashers; they hung on her every word.

'If venturing into the streets to do a little marketing, bring the pepper pot along. A would-be molester cannot achieve his evil purpose if temporarily blinded. Vinegar is also effective in this regard. If one arm is grasped, use the free hand and remove the hatpin. Sharp pain in any part of his person will compel the assailant to immediately desist. When kicking, if unable to aim for the male's most vulnerable area, aim for the shinbone. Nine times out of ten, the offender will raise the smarting leg and balance on one foot, thus enabling the intended victim to completely unbalance him. A shove is all it takes, better still a second kick, this time to the – being ladies, we'll call it the sit-upon. As well as putting the attacker on the ground, this has the added effect of causing embarrassment. Womanizers are cowards at heart and cannot bear embarrassment.'

The meeting closed on an optimistic note, Chloe Leeson and her friends wishing their instructress a warm welcome to Shayville and begging her to stay. She had fired their imagination; the hesitant were becoming downright militant.

'You've given us new hope, dear Mrs Tebbutt,' enthused Chloe. 'We won't forget the lessons you've taught us.'

'Remember, ladies,' urged Hattie. 'Practice, practice, practice.'

Wending their way homeward in good spirits, two
youngish women, both married, were accosted by a
couple of troopers and at once put their new
knowledge to the test. One retreated yelling in pain, a
hatpin stuck through his left earlobe. The other,
hopping on his right foot with his left shinbone
smarting, was kicked a second time and with such
gusto that he was driven forward, his forehead
making stunning contact with a lamp-post.

Toward 2am Rick rode out of Shayville, again
straddling the dapple and with the pickaxe and spade
secured to the saddle.

He blessed the obliging elements. It was pitch dark
until he reached the semi-circle of rocks. Cloudbanks
then rolled away from the moon, providing ample
light. He got to work with a will, digging, spading,
digging, spading and getting results. When the blade
of the shovel struck something unyielding, he tossed
it aside and began exploring with his bare hands.

Canvas. He knew the feel of canvas. A tarp had
been used to wrap whatever was buried here. He
grasped a fold of it and tugged at it, then sighted the
other wrapping. Oilskin. Before rummaging, he
paused, heaved a sigh and shook his head dazedly.

'Not luck,' he opined aloud. 'Providence.'

He fished out his jack-knife and, with its point, slit
some eighteen inches of oilskin. Replacing the knife
in his pocket, he lowered his hands to the slit and
parted it. Could this be? Still loath to believe it, he
took a chance, struck a match and held it low. No
mistake. His eyes were not deceiving him. He was
staring, until the match burned his fingertips, at part
of the barrel of a Gatling.

'Sorry, Vin,' was his next thought. 'You won't

appreciate being roused from sleep at so ungodly an hour – but you'll certainly appreciate what I have to tell you.'

He made sure the tarp was covering everything again before refilling the hole. A gentle breeze was blowing, invading the rock-bordered area, when he smoothed the disturbed earth and resecured his tools to the dapple. In fifteen minutes or less, all the marks of his having been here, his footprints, the hoofprints, would be erased.

Headed back to town, he pondered the enigma. It still didn't make sense. Why would Bearcat Webster leave the weapon cached there? With such a fearsome weapon his to use, he could have raised a lot of hell since removing it from the 3rd Cavalry's armoury.

Wait a minute.

What if the Gatling *had* been hijacked by whites? Webster could be unaware of its hiding place. But, no, this would mean Major Royle's suspicion was correct. He couldn't accept that. Major Royle right – about *anything*? Impossible. Unthinkable. Citizens of Shayville wearing moccasins, murdering a sergeant and trooper of the 3rd Cavalry, removing a Gatling gun from the Camp Kemp armoury? Never.

So where did that leave him? Well, he knew where it left the Gatling. Right there where he'd found it. And how long would it stay there, how long before the hijackers returned to retrieve it? He would have to move fast.

Fortunately, he had a plan.

Back in town, he stabled the dapple and hurried to the sheriff's office. Vin Strother would not be there, but the jailer bunked in the office or a cell. He rapped at the door until a bleary-eyed Curly Middlecott admitted him.

'Sorry about this, friend,' he apologized. 'But I have to talk to Vin rightaway. Where do I find him?'

'Hell's sakes, Chuck, he'll be asleep.'

'Not after I wake him. It's important.'

'Yeah, okay. Shipton's Room and Board on Tucker Road. He's in number seven.'

From the street doorway, the turnkey offered directions, and wondered how a man of Chuck Fairchild's years could scamper away at such speed.

The door of the building on Tucker Road was unlocked. Rick let himself in and followed a hallway dark and narrow, scratching matches to check door numbers. Reaching the door numbered 7, he turned the knob. Locked. No problem. He fished out his wallet, selected one of several short lengths of wire and began working on the lock. Minutes later, he was inside and closing the door behind him.

He lit the lamp, surveyed the room and reflected that the sheriff of Shay County had no taste for luxury. Not that this bedroom was untidy. It was just so austere, furnished with the bare essentials. The bed appeared none too comfortable. Plainly, Vin Strother didn't think so; he was snoring steadily. A closet, a small bedside table, a chair, a nail from which hung his belted Colt, a washbowl – and that was it.

Perching on the edge of the bed, he shook the lawman's shoulder. Strother came to his senses sluggishly, propped himself on an elbow and blinked at his unexpected visitor.

'Chuck. Holy Moses. You know what time it is?'

While Strother reached for his watch and squinted at it, Rick checked his own and said,

'Now we both know what time it is.'

'I guess you got a good reason. By damn, you *better* have.'

'You'll be interested in the reason, Vin. The stolen Gatling was cached, and I know where.'

An oath erupted from the sheriff. He quit his bed, trudged to the washbowl in his Long Johns, poured water from the pitcher, cupped his hands and scooped the water into his face. He spluttered, coughed, dried off with a tattered towel and planted himself in the chair.

'All right, I can see clear now, hear clear too. So tell me all about it.'

Still bedevilled by the time factor, Rick reported his find and the location as succinctly as he was able. He gave Strother a few moments to consider the significance of it before pressing his point home.

'Time could be working against us, Vin. We've no way of guessing how soon somebody'll show up to collect what they cached, so we have to act, and I mean immediately.'

'It all gets back to …' began Strother.

'Right,' nodded Rick. 'It gets back to my original suggestion – which appealed to you. The civilian law authority of this county has to return the gun to Camp Kemp and, if we move fast enough, you could also turn over to the commanding officer the rogues who stole it.'

'Webster's Arapahos, Chuck. Likely quite a passel of 'em.'

'Would Bearcat bring his whole force along to dig up the Gatling? Maybe not. Maybe no more than we can handle.'

'Who's we?'

'Well, how many reliable men can you recruit? We can count on both your deputies and I'll be with you as soon as I can make it.'

'I'd have to leave one deputy behind, Chuck.

What'll the citizens think if they can't find one tin star in town? The army's got all the authority, but ...'

'So you take one deputy along. Who else? Think carefully, Vin. They have to be hardheads, and it'd help if they resent the cavalry as much as you do. A fair-sized group could stake out in the timber east of the rocks. Ample concealment there for men and horses. They'll need to be well-armed and carrying a good supply of provisions, in case we have a long wait. Well, can you think of anybody?'

'There's only four I'd want to depend on,' muttered Strother. 'But they'll do fine. One of 'em'll be Bruno Hyatt, the blacksmith. And Jerry Kilburn'll want to be in it. He's a gunsmith.' He rose and moved to the window. 'You savvy what you're asking? To reach that timber before sun-up, I got to move *now*, rouse those men, get provisioned up and ...'

'You have time enough,' insisted Rick.

'Just about,' decided Strother. 'And you'll come join us, huh?'

'For sure,' Rick said firmly. 'Best chance we'll ever get. I crave to be in on the action.'

'Figure you're strong enough?' frowned Strother. Then he remembered. 'Oh, sure. Self-whatever-you-call-it, the stuff you learned from Injun medicine men.'

'I aim to do my share,' Rick assured him, as he rose to leave.

He checked his watch again while quitting Shipton's. It displeased him to admit to himself that he was weary now, but he had to be practical. What sleep he could have between now and when he left to join the Strother party at the stakeout, he needed it; in a showdown, a half-awake man is worse than useless.

It did not occur to him to remove his disguise when he retired; he just flopped on his bed and fell into deep slumber.

At nine a.m., Major Royle was glaring at his second-in-command from behind his desk. Lieutenant Clive Purvis was young, scrupulously polite to senior officers and by no means handsome, plain-faced in fact. He was also a shrewd man skilled at masking his feelings, which was just as well. He could read Royle like an open book and secretly regarded him as an insufferable blowhard painfully lacking in tact and, for that matter, common sense.

'Six more troopers on the sick list, unfit for duty?' gasped Royle. 'Impossible! I refuse to believe it!'

'Begging the major's pardon,' Purvis respectfully countered, 'the major has no choice but to believe it, for it is all sadly true.'

'In a brawl with loutish minehands, troopers of B Company should emerge victorious and unscathed,' insisted Royle.

'As to the disturbance in front of the meeting hall, four troopers in conflict with three minehands ...' Purvis, an inveterate note-taker, produced and opened a notebook. 'Four versus three, yes, we can conclude our men emerged as the victors. But unscathed? I fear not, sir.'

'Those details again, Lieutenant.'

'Yes, sir. One soldier, a broken collarbone, two soldiers, rib injuries, the fourth soldier, a fractured jaw and one broken arm.'

'And the other two?'

'Sorry, sir. Three. I'm forgetting Trooper Biddolph, who apparently attempted to board a moving buggy. The driver was a lady who, obviously

resenting Trooper Biddolph's action, struck him with
some object, a furled umbrella I would imagine, with
the result that the trooper fell. The buggy horse *may*
have stomped him. In any event, he's laid up with a
dislocated shoulder. And the other two ...'

'Injured by *women*?'

'Well, Major, a hatpin had to be removed from
Trooper Jackson's ear. Male citizens do not have any
use for hatpins, so we're forced to assume ...'

'Stabbed through the ear by a confounded hatpin?'

'A painful experience for him I'm sure. And
Trooper Finn, though concussed, recalls being kicked
twice by a lady, the second kick causing him to butt a
post.'

'This is absolutely outlandish and unpardonable!'
stormed the major. 'Are the women of this
community losing their minds?'

'I have made certain inquiries,' offered Purvis. 'It
seems the ladies of Shayville are organizing. The
brawl between four of our men and three minehands
was caused by the ejection of said minehands from
the meeting hall. They were simply thrown out,
thrown some distance, so the ladies who did so must
have been quite strong – as well as indignant.'

Royle's eyebrows shot up.

'Are you telling me a meeting was held?'

'Inaugural meeting, chaired by Mrs Leeson, of a
group of ladies dedicating themselves to self-
defence.'

'B Company provides all the protection Shayville
women may require, Lieutenant Purvis,' snapped
Royle.

'With respect, sir, the ladies apparently feel a need
to defend themselves against their defenders. Or, to
put it another way, they complain of being molested

by as many troopers as minehands. The organization is to be known as the LRC. I believe that stands for Ladies Reform Committee.'

'And Leeson's wife masterminded this scheme?' grinned Royle, twirling his moustache. 'Ah hah! Now I have them! A breach of martial law!'

'I don't quite follow …'

'You should, Lieutenant. If you're missing my point, consult the relevant manual. Where martial law is in force, mere civilians, male or female, cannot hold public meetings without the permission of the officer in charge. The fool woman requested no such permission of me, therefore I have her by the bustle!'

'Do you consider this a serious offence, sir?' frowned Purvis.

'Don't you?' challenged Royle.

'I don't mean to speak out of turn, sir.' The lieutenant appealed to reason, but in vain. 'But surely you realize the conduct of some of our men here in Shayville has been – well – less than gentlemanly. I mean, where the ladies are concerned.'

'Balderdash,' snorted Royle. 'A lot of nervous biddies, wives of local men hostile to the army.' He rose and reached for his hat. 'I'll put a stop to this nonsense immediately. How dare the Leeson woman conspire against me! Well, by thunder, she'll learn her lesson. When I'm through quoting army regulations to her, she'll wish she'd never devised such a scheme. The LRC will be disbanded this very day!'

He began leaving, but Purvis delayed him a few moments.

'Just a thought, sir.'

'Yes, Lieutenant?'

'With our Shayville casualties increasing, the local

doctors must be overworked. They are, after all, attending army personnel as well as injured miners and civilians. Might it not be advisable to apprise Colonel Cobcroft of the situation and request that Surgeon Major McBain be moved into town to ease the ...?'

'Certainly not!' Royle's complexion changed to beetroot-red. 'An irresponsible suggestion, Lieutenant! My authority as commander of the company billeted here is under challenge, and *I* will deal with that challenge! On no account is the colonel to be informed of our casualties – is that clear?'

'As the major wishes,' nodded Purvis.

Ben Leeson and spouse had just finished breakfast when, without knocking, Royle entered their temporary home, marched into their parlour and said his piece – truculently, triumphantly. Leeson was impassive at the start, his wife intimidated by Royle's accusation.

'You are guilty, madam, of breaching martial law. I will impose no penalty, but let it be clearly understood there are to be no more meetings of your organization.'

'Oh, my!' flinched Chloe.

'To have called such a meeting without my written consent is a serious offence!' boomed Royle. 'I give you until mid-afternoon of this day to contact the women you recruited and advise them that the LRC is officially disbanded!'

'Major,' said Leeson. 'My wife isn't deaf. You're talking to just two people in a small parlour, not a public gathering, so I'll thank you not to bellow at us. And since when does the United States Cavalry fear an organization of civilians of the so-called weaker sex?'

'They are taking advantage of their womanhood, Leeson,' growled Royle, 'by deliberately assaulting troopers under my command, troopers whose chivalry prevents their defending themselves.'

'That's not exactly what's been happening,' retorted Leeson. 'Your troopers're out of hand. If you don't know that, you just aren't keeping your official eye on them.'

'I am not here to bandy words with you,' snapped Royle.

'In my own home – humble though it is, compared to our quarters in *my* hotel which you now occupy – I'll bandy words with you or any other bigmouth who intrudes on us,' declared Leeson.

'Still sulking, Leeson?' sneered Royle. 'Hate to admit it, don't you? Those riff raff *civilian* miners would be running roughshod over this town were it not policed by B Company.'

'You should try policing your own men,' warned Leeson. 'I'm not much of a fighter, Major, but I can only be pushed so far, so you'd better believe the next brave soldier who offends my wife is gonna feel my boot on his cavalry blue backside.'

'Benjamin!' breathed Chloe.

'Madam, you have my orders,' scowled Royle.

And marched out, slamming the front door behind him, leaving the Leesons frowning at each other.

'It seemed such a sensible idea,' sighed Chloe. 'Well, good heavens, *somebody* had to do *something*, and I truly believed we ladies had a right to take action.'

'It was one of your better ideas,' said Leeson. 'I thought so when you mentioned it to me and I still think so.'

'All for nothing,' she complained. 'And it was such a successful first meeting, especially after that wonderful Mrs Tebbutt addressed us and – and gave demonstrations, started teaching us to protect ourselves. Oh, Ben, this is terrible. They'll be so disappointed. There was such enthusiasm!'

'Mrs Tebbutt sounds like quite a lady.' Leeson had made a shrewd guess as to the true identity of Mrs Tebbutt. 'Just what the group needed.'

'What a letdown,' frowned Chloe. 'I'll have to start calling on them rightaway and – I can think of several ladies who'll want to defy the major's orders.'

'As long as you have to look 'em up, why don't you look in on Mrs Tebbutt first?' he suggested. 'You never can tell. Smart lady like her. Maybe she'll figure out some kind of counter-move.'

'She's such a comforting person, and so wise,' said Chloe. 'Yes, that's what I'll do. I'll go straight to her and tell her everything.'

Rick had slept late and found it necessary to make repairs to his disguise before hurrying to the dining room, barely made it in time for breakfast. Now he was with Hattie in her room, she listening to his bragging with an indulgent smile.

'Tremendous progress, darling,' she commented.

'Well ...' He decided to be modest, 'freak luck and providence, one chance in a thousand. I'd be a liar if I claimed I *expected* to find the Gatling there.'

'And, by now,' she surmised, 'Sheriff Strother and his volunteers are keeping the cache under observation. So, sooner or later, something's bound to break.'

'My money's on some of Bearcat's braves, maybe with Bearcat himself in charge,' he muttered wistfully. 'That, my dear, would be just perfect. We seize them *and* the gun and take them to the Third Cavalry headquarters. Beautiful. And Colonel Cobcroft would have to be of superior intelligence to

Major Bighead Royle. A nose-picking fourteen-year-old with pimples would be superior in intellect to Royle.'

'Royle does seem – quite incredible.'

'He *is* incredible. Hattie love, if I hadn't visited the jackass, seen him in the flesh, I wouldn't believe he exists.'

A knock at the door. Rick got up and backstepped to the window.

'Who?' called Hattie.

'Mrs Tebbutt, it's Chloe Leeson. I must speak with you. Something terrible has happened!'

'Won't keep you a moment.' Hattie jerked a thumb and, as Rick began making his exit via the window, blew him a kiss. She then moved to the door to unlock and open it and welcome her visitor. 'Good morning, Mrs Leeson. How nice of you to call.'

In the back alley, Rick propped a shoulder against the section of wall between his wife's and his own window; he had decided to eavesdrop.

Chloe accepted a chair and gave vent to her distress, reporting Major Royle's visit, his harangue and his demands almost word for word with Hattie nodding sympathetically.

'I'm just not ready to face the members,' Chloe said tremulously. 'How can I tell them – after all our wonderful plans …?'

'It's a bitter disappointment,' agreed Hattie.

'I don't know who to turn to – except you, dear Mrs Tebbutt. It was my husband's suggestion. He thought, being such a clever person, you might think of – well – a way *around* our problem.'

'I'm flattered by your husband's confidence in me.'

'I too have confidence in you. You won our trust last night, our admiration.'

'There is one chance,' frowned Hattie.

'You've thought of something already?' Chloe brightened considerably.

'I doubt the major would listen to me, an ageing woman he'd probably dismiss as an old fussbudget,' said Hattie. 'But my daughter can be quite persuasive, dear girl that she is.'

'You have a daughter – here in Shayville?' asked Chloe.

'Staying at a better hotel,' Hattie told her. 'We're devoted to each other. She's a fine and loyal daughter, but she has expensive tastes. It's not unusual for us to register at separate hotels.' She smiled fondly. 'So beautiful. Her father, my late husband Clarence, would have been so proud. And such a strong personality.'

'Inherited from you, I'm sure,' said Chloe. 'And you think she …?'

'Well, as I said, Lucinda can be quite persuasive. I'll explain the situation to her, and I've no doubt she'll offer to visit Major Royle and – talk to him. It may help.'

'I pray that it will.'

'Be optimistic, Mrs Leeson. Go home and hope for the best. Meanwhile, I'll go see Lucinda and we'll arrange something.'

Chloe Leeson departed in better spirits, cheered by Hattie's assurances. When Rick climbed through the window again, his wife had opened her trunk and was choosing a change of garb.

'You snooped,' she guessed.

'I'm in the snooping business,' he reminded her. 'I take it, resourceful spouse of mine, you're about to break in a new act?'

'Showtime again,' she said briskly. 'From what you've told me of the major, it's obvious conceit is his big weakness.'

'One of them,' he nodded. 'He has so many. His imagination, for instance, has no sense of direction.'

'I think I know how to capitalize on a man's weaknesses.'

'I'll vouch for that. So Lucinda Tebbutt's about to make her entrance? Good thinking, honey, but don't overdo it with Royle. Remember you're a married woman with an insanely jealous husband.'

'Thanks for the reminder.' Hattie removed her wedding band.

'What're you gonna be?' he asked, as she checked her collection of wigs. 'A redhead?'

'The black wig,' she decided. 'Black-haired women have a sensuous, smouldering quality.'

'Royle will probably catch fire,' he predicted.

'Off with the old lady make-up,' she mused. 'Darken the eyebrows. The right gown of course. Snug-fitting with a low neckline. A discreet application of the right perfume.'

'My favourite,' he grinned. 'Frantic Desire.'

'Just Desire,' she corrected. 'You're the only one calls it Frantic Desire.'

'I have my reasons,' he winked.

'You'd better get out of here,' she chuckled.

'Time I was on my way,' he agreed. 'Vin and his volunteers'll be waiting for me.' He retreated to the window. 'Knock 'em dead, sweetheart. Too bad I'll be gone before Lucinda makes her first appearance. That'd be something to see. All the luck.'

'You too,' she said. 'And, if your business with Sheriff Strother and the hijackers can't be a peaceful negotiation, for heaven's sake keep your head down. I need you, darling.'

'The feeling's mutual. Be seeing you.'

# 5

# The Heavy Feminine Touch

Rick's exit from Shayville was as unobtrusive as he could manage; the same would not be said of Lucinda Tebbutt's first and only appearance a short time after his departure.

As well as his shoulder-holstered pistol, he wore his Colt .45 with his coat buttoned. He stopped by the Glad Hand before proceeding to Devoy's to again rent the dapple. Arlo Coventry accepted his plea; a rheumatic condition would necessitate his taking to his bed for an indefinite period, but he would be back on duty in due course.

He also thought to purchase a few provisions. At the Devoy barn, the dapple was saddled for him. He left by way of the west back alley and rode a half-circle around the county seat, then started east for the rendezvous.

He was well on his way when, in her room, Hattie put the finishing touches to her Lucinda Tebbutt persona and studied her reflection in a mirror.

The gown was just right, she decided. Maroon satin and clinging in all the right places, accentuating the positive, specifically her trim waistline, rounded hips and eye-catching bosom, just enough cleavage to accelerate male puberty, possibly causing males of advanced years to regret their advanced years. Perched atop the lustrous black hair was a mere confection of a chapeau, colourful, frivolous. She had been sparing with make-up, needed only the blackening of her brows and discreet application of lip rouge; her flawless complexion complemented her other facial assets.

A purse, a reticule? No, just a parasol. And furled.

She restored her old lady get-up and her make-up box to the trunk and locked it. After locking her door, she moved to the window. Better to leave by the window. Leaving or entering through the lobby, only *Mrs* Tebbutt should be seen.

A few passers-by in the back alley. She waited till backs were turned to her before climbing out. The window was lowered, but not locked. To the north rear corner of the hotel she walked, then into the side alley giving access to Main Street.

She then began her jaunty, graceful saunter northward toward the Grand Hotel, and Main Street wasn't quite the same for some time thereafter. The most beautiful woman ever seen in Shayville was at once the target of all eyes. She was gawked at, appraised, ogled by every citizen in sight, especially those of masculine gender. Nobody accosted her, but there were incidents, side effects of her uptown promenade. In its time, Shayville had experienced a distraction or two, but Hattie, alias Lucinda, was the ultimate.

A workman half way up a ladder was following her movements through dilated eyes. As she passed, he twisted to catch a rear view, overbalanced and fell; she hoped he suffered no serious injury.

The driver of a buckboard turned his rig to give his eyes a treat and collided with a surrey whose driver was also gaping.

On the opposite side of the street, a storekeeper sweeping the sidewalk in front of his premises worked his broom faster, his eyes fixed on the black-haired beauty. On the upswing, the business end of the broom struck the posterior of a female pedestrian of ample proportions walking past at that moment of moments. In outraged indignation, the woman clobbered him with her parasol.

As though oblivious to her effect on the local population, Hattie serenely continued on her way.

A half block along, again on the east side of Main, a saloonkeeper thrust his head out his upstairs window for an intent appraisal of the gorgeous brunette. He planted his hands on the window ledge and leaned further out, and further, became top-heavy, lost his balance and pitched out head-first to crash on and demolish the ground floor awning. But this didn't stop him. He rose sore-headed and bloody-nosed from the wreckage, limped to the outer edge of the sidewalk and kept right on staring.

The last townsman Hattie passed before reaching the steps of the Grand Hotel was a professional gambler pausing to light a cigar. Being a veteran of the green baize tables, he prided himself on being one cool hombre. He looked her over, but impassively, then lit his cigar, inserted the dead match in his mouth and tossed the cigar away.

Hattie climbed the steps and entered the lobby. Five troopers and one corporal were idling there until she crossed the threshold to dynamic effect. They became goggle-eyed. The trooper lounging in a tilted chair brought his feet up too fast. The chair toppled and so did he.

The corporal presented himself to the vision with his eyes glazed and his Adam's apple bobbing.

'Uh – ma'am ...?'

'Not ma'am,' she corrected, treating him to a smile. The smile and a whiff of her perfume won a gulp from him. 'The name is Tebbutt, Miss Lucinda Tebbutt. I do so wish to speak to Major Royle. Please tell me he's not too busy.'

The speech pattern she affected was low, husky, caressing. 'He ain't too busy,' mumbled the noncom. 'He won't be – I mean he won't *wanta* be – not when he gets an eyeful – I mean not when he sees you. This way, Miss.'

He led her to the stairs. As they began climbing, he stumbled. By the time they reached the top floor, he had stumbled three times. It could have been four times; Hattie wasn't keeping count.

They arrived at the closed door of the major's quarters.

'Please announce me,' she urged.

'Uh – yeah – that's what I'll do,' he nodded. 'I'll announce you.'

He knocked and entered, closed the door behind him and advanced so hastily that he tripped on the edge of a rug and ended up half-sprawled across Royle's desk. Royle glowered.

'Corporal, what the devil's the matter with you?' he demanded. 'Are you drunk?'

'No, Major sir. But, after this, I'm gonna need a shiff stot of rye.'

'*What* did you say?'

'Stiff shot of rye. Whiskey, sir. On accounta I'm all shook.'

'Make sense, man!'

'I'm announcin' her, sir. Meanin' the lady.'

'I presume she has a name?'

'Tebbutt.'

'Ah hah! A familiar name now. The old biddy inciting other old biddies of Shayville to assault and battery on my garrison.'

'Beggin' the major's pardon. This ain't no old biddy. She's ...' The corporal intoned the name with reverence. And trembled. 'Miss – Lucinda – Tebbutt.'

'Why are you shaking, confound you?' challenged Royle.

'Sir, I never saw a gal so – well – she is some helluva looker.'

'Her looks will cut no ice with me, Corporal,' declared Royle. 'I'm a professional soldier who can't be swayed by *any* woman. You may send her in, but warn her I can spare only two minutes, understand?'

'Yes, sir.' Returning to the corridor, the corporal gawked at Hattie. 'Major'll give you just two minutes, Miss.'

He froze as she smiled, straightened his headgear and murmured,

'Want to bet?'

She hadn't lost her touch, knew how to make an entrance with maximum effect. Royle was treated to a hippy strut, then a bedazzling smile, then a jaunty advance to his desk with the door closing behind her. Royle's eyes bulged. He jerked upright, stared at her incredulously and with the extremities of his waxed moustache quivering.

'Major Calvin Cornelius Royle – your servant, Miss Lucinda!'

'My, oh my.' She fluttered her eyelashes. 'Such gallantry. But can a lady expect less from an officer and a gentleman?'

'Please be seated,' he invited. 'No, that chair isn't comfortable enough. Allow me, dear lady.'

'Please don't trouble.' She said this a minute and a half later, during which time he removed the chair fronting his desk and made heavy going of trying to replace it with the one by the window. In the process, he caught a leg of it in the drapes and almost brought them down. Her two minutes, she was thinking, were almost up. 'Make *yourself* comfortable, Major dear. I'll sit here.'

She perched on the right side of the desk and crossed her legs. Royle abandoned his fight to the death with the drapes and hurried back to his chair. He was sweating now. Melting pomade dribbled down past his sideburns.

'How may I serve you?' He pleaded, and feverishly. 'Anything, Miss Lucinda. I'm yours to command.'

'It's just a teensy little thing,' she smiled. 'I'm almost ashamed to bother you about it, but Mother is just *so* distressed, wondering what you must *think* of her. Why, Major dear, she'd just *die* if you disapproved of her little contribution to the safety of the ladies of Shayville.'

'I – uh – well ...' he began.

She leaned closer to him. His head spun, his eyes rolled.

'It's such a shame that some of those poor darlings hurt some of your trooper boys,' she cooed. 'But then boys will be boys, you agree? And men will be men and, sometimes, they do forget their manners.' Raising and waggling a forefinger, she switched from cooing to wheedling. 'And, when they accost the ladies, it's so terrifying for them. So, if no brave gentleman comes to their aid, they just have to defend themselves. That's all Mother is teaching them. Just self-defence, Major dear. Believe me, she wouldn't *dream* of declaring war on the United States Cavalry.'

'Your mother …' Royle was struggling to regain his composure, 'must be a remarkable lady.'

'She thinks *I'm* remarkable,' she murmured.

'So do I!' he gasped.

'Now, Major dear …' she chuckled.

'Remarkable – astonishing – unbelievably beautiful!'

'My, oh my. Such flattery.'

'Dinner this evening?' he begged. 'I'll commandeer the best restaurant in town and – and hire musicians. We'll dine by candlelight. I'll forbid the proprietor to admit anybody else. We'll have the place to ourselves, just the two of us.'

'Please, no more.' She heaved a sigh. 'This is so sad. By evening, I'll be gone. Mother is staying, but I have to leave on the afternoon coach. There are women in another town desperately needing to be taught the Hardnut methods of self-defence. I'm just *devastated*, Major dear. It would have been such a marvellous evening for me – an evening neither of us would ever forget.'

'Cancel your passage,' he pleaded. 'Just don't go.'

'I'm committed, so I *must* go,' she said forlornly. 'But, Calvin – I may call you Calvin …?'

'*Please*, Lucinda!'

'I could perhaps – return to Shayville – to you.'

'As quickly as possible! Yes, come back! I'll be waiting!'

Hattie was reflecting, 'I'm glad I didn't write this dialogue. It's so crass – I'd never forgive myself.'

'However,' she frowned.

'However – yes?' he asked.

'We seem to have become distracted, Calvin dear.'
She treated him to another smile; his blood pressure
skyrocketted. 'I came here to plead with you. Not to –
be overcome – as I believe you too are overcome.'

'I'm overcome,' he earnestly assured her.

'To plead with you on Mother's behalf, on behalf of
all those worried women who ask no more than to be
allowed to prepare for the worst,' she said. 'Dearest
Calvin, the worst could happen. They are so
defenceless. I'm sure you do your best, but you have
so many responsibilities. How can you provide for
their protection while – doing everything else that's
expected of you, apprehending the murderers who
stole all that gold and those bloodthirsty savages led
by that *awful* renegade, that Webster person? I'm so
concerned. It all seems too much for you, so tiring.'

'I am tireless,' he insisted.

'And to think ...' She gestured helplessly, 'he's
called Webster. Oh, the bitter *irony* of it! Why couldn't
he be like his namesake, Noah Webster, and do
something useful and productive, such as compiling a
dictionary?'

'I'll bring Webster to justice,' he vowed. 'None of
them can outwit me, the fiends who massacred the
prospectors, the fiends who seized the Gatling – none
of them.'

'Meanwhile, Calvin dearest, you *will* permit Mother
to continue her good work, won't you?' She reached
for his hand; his nerves jumped. 'You'll rescind your
ban on the LRC. She was desperate when she begged
me to intercede for her. It means so much to her.
She'll be heartbroken.'

'I'll revoke the ban,' he announced. 'You may tell
her I've reconsidered and the ladies are welcome to
resume their meetings.'

'I *knew* you'd understand,' she breathed, and patted his cheek. 'The moment our eyes met, Calvin, I said to myself "Here is an officer and a gentleman, intelligent, understanding, compassionate". She'll be so grateful.' She slid from the desk. 'I must tell her at once. And – when I return to Shayville ...'

'I'll be counting the hours,' he mumbled.

She blew him a kiss. He rose to stare after her, to commit to memory every inch of her anatomy, as she moved to the door and opened it. She threw a last radiant smile over her shoulder before making her exit.

'P.T. Barnum,' she was thinking as she quit the hotel. 'You are so right. There *is* one born every minute, and they grow up to become Calvin Royles.'

Her ten-minute journey to her room at the Kirkland House was low profile. She spared Main Street further disruption and risk to life and limb of male citizenry by using the west alley. When she reached her window, she waited patiently for passers-by to pass on by before raising it and climbing in.

Lowering the shade, she removed the frivolous headgear, the black wig and the gown and again rigged the changes. A short time later, 'Mrs Elmira Tebbutt' presented herself at the reception desk, proffered her key and requested directions to the home of Mayor and Mrs Leeson.

This promenade along Main Street was an orderly progress. Only ladies now acquainted with her, devoted followers, smiled and nodded to her. Traffic along Main moved smoothly. The workman was back on his ladder and in no danger of losing his balance. Men didn't gawk. Nobody fell from a second story window.

'Oh, well,' Hattie reflected. 'That's show business.'

At the Leeson home, Chloe anxiously admitted her and introduced her to her husband.

'My pleasure, Mrs Tebbutt,' said Leeson, hoping she wouldn't notice his searching appraisal. 'My wife speaks highly of you.'

'What news?' frowned Chloe. 'Was your daughter able to – influence the major?'

'Quite successfully,' smiled Hattie. 'The crisis is over, Mrs Leeson. Well, I did say Lucinda can be quite persuasive, did I not? Major Royle has reconsidered. We have his permission to hold further meetings. The LRC has his official approval.'

'This is wonderful news!' cried Chloe. 'Oh, I'm so relieved, so grateful to your daughter!'

'You should prove your gratitude by inviting Mrs Tebbutt and her daughter to have supper with us tonight,' Leeson suggested, still studying Hattie.

'Could you ...?' begged Chloe.

'Your invitation is much appreciated, but I must decline,' said Hattie. 'Lucinda leaves today and, this evening, I must consult the manual.'

'The manual?' asked Chloe.

'Prepared by Miranda Hardnut, complete with diagrams,' explained Hattie. 'It's important, you see, that I refresh my memory of her lessons, the special instructions, the techniques, so that our next meeting will really be a class, a training session. We dare not relax, Mrs Leeson. Our problems won't resolve themselves. We must practice, practice, practice.'

'Of course,' Chloe eagerly agreed.

'You're kind of overstrung, Chloe,' remarked the mayor. 'Why don't you go lie down, rest a while? I'll see Mrs Tebbutt out.'

Chloe hugged Hattie emotionally and withdrew,

leaving her husband to usher their visitor out and down the walk to the front gate. There, he grinned blandly, expressed his regret that both Mrs Tebbutt and her persuasive daughter could not be their supper guests this night. With a knowing wink, he assured her he did realize this would be a physical impossibility. Hattie responded in her old lady voice.

'Discretion, Mayor Leeson. I'm pleased you appreciate the efforts of two certain parties, but I feel bound to remind you ...'

'Strict secrecy,' he nodded. 'Don't ever worry on my account. I won't run off at the mouth, not even to Chloe. Got too much riding on this deal. So I'll just say those two certain parties are sure earning what they'll be paid. Well, one other thing I want to say. If your daughter's as beautiful as a lady I met in Denver just recently, I'm not surprised she charmed Major Royle out of his muddled little mind.'

Hattie dropped her voice, her natural voice.

'Confidentially, he's a sucker for French perfume and a little feminine flim flam.'

From within the timber east of the temporary burial place of a fearsome weapon, only four men watched the rider they knew as Julius 'Chuck' Fairchild approaching from the west.

Sheriff Strother had anticipated backing from five trusty helpers. The only three with him were Deputy Roy Bass, the brawny, grizzle-haired Bruno Hyatt, a blacksmith, and the wiry, sharp-featured gunsmith, Jerry Kilburn.

Rick, well and truly in character, idled the dapple around the rocks and on into the timber where they awaited him; the clearing was just wide enough and well-concealed.

'Chuck.' Strother nodded affably. 'Figured you'd show around now.'

Dismounting, tying his horse with the others, Rick was conscious of the intent scrutiny of Hyatt and Kilburn. He was careful about his movements. Not too brisk, as befitted a man of his supposed years. As he trudged across to squat with the foursome, the sheriff performed introductions.

'You already know Roy. Like I said, we had to leave Billy in town. The big feller's Bruno Hyatt, a tad short on temper, but good at followin' orders. The other 'un's Jerry Kilburn, a right smart gunsmith. Come to think of it, he can be as ornery as Bruno. Boys, this's the gent I've been tellin' you about. Say howdy to Chuck Fairchild.'

'Bruno – Jerry ...'

Rick offered his hand. Shaking with him, Hyatt and Kilburn noted his firm grip.

'Damned if I savvy it,' growled the blacksmith. 'Vin's talked of that mumbo jumbo you got taught by some Injun, but I don't savvy it nohow. Don't seem nachral for a gent your age to be so frisky.'

'You know, Chuck,' frowned Kilburn. 'There's no guessing how this thing's gonna work out. Could be a whole party of Arapahos headed this way any time. You sure you can keep up with us?'

'You any good with that six-shooter?' demanded Hyatt.

Rick drew his Colt, twirled it by the trigger guard and deftly reholstered it. He then allowed them a glimpse of his shoulder-holstered .38.

'Guns and me,' he drawled. 'Old friends from way back. And, speaking of guns ...'

'It's still there,' Bass assured him, and gestured to the spade slung to a charcoal's saddle. 'Bruno checked. Don't fret, Chuck. Time he was through, the ground looked just like before he started diggin'.'

'Perfect setup, Vin,' Rick remarked, gazing about. 'Won't be anybody spot us, but we'll sight riders headed this way from any direction. Only five of us, but there's a lot five good men can do when the chips're down.'

'I was countin' on seven,' grouched Strother.

He went on to report that one of the men he had wanted to recruit was being treated for colic by one of Shayville's overworked medicos. The wife of the other was expecting their first child.

'Like they say,' Rick shrugged unconcernedly, 'them's the breaks.'

'We fetched plenty provisions along,' said Bass.

Which reminded the gunsmith.

'Us five better stay friendly. Vin warned Bruno and me. No guessing how long we'll be stuck here, just waiting.'

'Be of good heart, my friend,' smiled Rick. 'I'm in no doubt we're a congenial quintet.'

'I got a feelin' in my water, strong hunch we won't be idle more'n a couple days,' muttered the deputy. 'Damn devil-gun's been cached there since it was grabbed from the Camp Kemp armoury by them renegades. How much longer'll Bearcat wait to move it to the Laberinto Hills? Hell, he stole it to *use* it. So I'm bettin' a couple days at most.'

'And how many bucks'll he fetch along?' wondered Hyatt.

'As many as we can outfight – let's hope,' Rick said calmly. 'So, Vin, what of our fire-power?'

'We're all packin' pistols, you're totin' two,' said Strother. 'Us four got rifles too, and Bruno fetched his shotgun along.'

'And we got plenty ammunition,' declared Bass.

'So let 'em come – no matter how many.' Rick's old man speech was soft, but resolute. 'With those trees for cover, we can throw enough lead at those rocks to defeat double our number. This is a secret stakeout, which gives us the all-important edge, gentlemen. Day or night, because we can live without coffee or hot meals for as long as it takes – so there'll be no cookfire, no smoke to alert marauders of our presence.'

Being a gunsmith by profession, Kilburn could and did make his next point with authority.

'Any redmen caught in those rocks'll be at a disadvantage, to put it mildly. Any kind of bullet bounces off a hard surface – rock for instance – it ricochets, screaming, and stopping a ricocheting bullet's the worst thing can happen to a man. It's not just a slug any more. It's splayed, all jagged, but still travelling fast. Ask any doctor. Drawing any kind of bullet from a casualty is a rough chore. Digging out a ricocheted bullet is murder.'

'Uh huh, sure,' grunted Hyatt. 'But, when the shootin' starts, I won't be feeling' merciful, not so you'd notice. I'll be thinkin' about how much blood an Injun could spill, cuttin' loose at whites with a damn Gatlin'.'

'Gentlemen, I don't believe tobacco will give us away, certainly not in daylight,' said Rick, delving into his pockets. 'So I brought extra cigars along.'

'Genuine Havanas,' Hyatt eagerly noted.

'For my gallant comrades, nothing but the best,' Rick said amiably.

Mid-morning of the next day, while Vin Strother and his small force were still waiting it out, one of them with a telescope pointed south to the Laberinto Hills, the Leesons received another visitor.

Elias Jacklin, wealthiest mining speculator of the region, was big, florid, assertive and expensively tailored. He was not, however, as bumptious as a certain officer of the 3rd Cavalry. He did knock and, when admitted by the mayor's wife, bared his head and addressed her respectfully.

'Like to talk to your husband, Mrs Leeson, if he's here.'

'You're most welcome, Mister Jacklin,' she smiled. 'This way to the parlour.'

He won a cordial greeting from Leeson and accepted a comfortable chair, after which he aired his grievance. Too many of his hired hands were laid up with injuries, many inflicted by *women* for the love of Mike. With so many employees unfit for work, production was slowing down. He couldn't afford such a reversal, having invested considerable cash in his enterprises.

'So, as mayor of Shayville ...' He eyed Leeson reproachfully, 'wouldn't you say it's high time you did something about that covey of quails who've been putting my men on the sick list?'

'I guess you mean the LRC,' said Leeson. 'The Ladies Reform Committee.'

'Whatever they call themselves,' Jacklin said irritably. 'I don't know who organized them, but ...'

'May I present Madam Chairwoman?' grinned Leeson, nodding to Chloe.

Jacklin blinked at her.

'No offence, Mrs Leeson.'

'We're a self-defence committee,' she explained.

'Fine, sure,' said Jacklin. 'But I'm still protesting. I mean, it all has to stop. Somebody has to *do* something.'

'There is much you could do, Mister Jacklin,' said Chloe. 'I'm surprised it hasn't occurred to you. Our dear friend Mrs Tebbutt is continuing with the lessons, so our confidence is increasing, also our ability to protect ourselves. Undoubtedly there will be more minehands laid off work unless you take the obvious step.'

'Me?' frowned Jacklin.

'The ladies only injure men taking liberties with them,' she pointed out. 'We don't go looking for victims, Mister Jacklin. We'd never descend to unprovoked assault. Dear me, no.'

'There's something *I* can do?' he challenged.

'Well now,' said Leeson. 'You're the most successful mine boss in all Shay County – therefore the most influential.'

'*Use* your influence, and your authority,' urged Chloe. 'If you can convince your own employees and the whole mining fraternity to refrain from molesting the ladies of Shayville, you'd do much to ease the situation. Not too much to ask, surely?'

'Well …' began Jacklin.

'All *we* ask,' she stressed, 'is the right to walk out of our homes and venture into the streets of *our* town without fear of being set upon by roughnecks.'

'Nobody expects minehands to be angels,' Leeson assured Jacklin. 'But, you know, certain standards of conduct should be maintained.'

Jacklin digested the suggestion, rose from his chair and had the good grace to declare to Chloe,

'You're absolutely right, Mrs Leeson. The idea *should've* occurred to me. My apologies. Pressure of business – you know how it is. Not that that's any excuse. It certainly *is* up to me to warn my crew to behave themselves, and I'll pass on the advice to all the other mining outfits.'

He thanked the Leesons and was ushered out. After he had left, the mayor grinned encouragingly.

'Progress, honey. We're getting somewhere. The tide's gradually turning.'

'Thanks to Mrs Tebbutt,' insisted Chloe. 'Where would we be without her? The situation could only have worsened.'

'Keep up the good work,' said Leeson. 'And let's be optimistic. There'll come a time when we can move out of here and back to our comfortable suite at the hotel.'

'I want that so much,' she sighed. 'But it seems too much to hope for.'

'Believe me,' he said. 'It's *not* too much to hope for.'

Afternoon of this day, soon after the county school closed, a pretty thirteen-year-old girl making her way homeward along Main Street caught the eye of a trooper, Lawson by name. In his cups and feeling raunchy, he accosted her. The girl froze in fear and the confrontation was witnessed by that 'old biddy' Mrs Elmira Tebbutt, but also by Deputy Billy Grimble, who happened to be closer.

Crossing the street at a run, Grimble arrived to give vent to his disgust.

'Take your stinkin' paws off of her, soldier-boy,' he growled, and snapped his fingers. '*This* for martial law! I got a mind to give you what you're beggin' for – a cell in the county jail! By damn, I'll *do* it! You're under arrest! I'm takin' you in!'

The scene was being enacted in front of a hardware store. The next building north was the saloon from which Lawson had emerged. And now, just as Hattie arrived, two other troopers moved out of the saloon and advanced on the deputy threateningly.

'You and who else, star-packer?' one of them challenged with a leer.

'Dear child,' Hattie said softly, reassuringly. 'Go along home.'

The girl needed no second bidding, took to her heels. Then, to Grimble's consternation, Hattie drew a pickaxe handle from the barrel by the store entrance – and hefted it.

'Reprobates! Blackguardly lechers!' she cried.

And began swinging.

# 6

# Making an Impression

For some little time, Deputy Billy Grimble was one very confused lawman.

Nothing wrong with his eyesight. No youngster, this peppery old lady wielding a pickaxe handle. So gently she had reassured the badly scared girl, but so ferociously did she set to with that commandeered club. He was fascinated, could only stand and gape.

The drunken trooper who had accosted the girl was Hattie's first target. He began ducking, but not fast enough. Struck above the right ear, he parted company with the sidewalk, toppling off it to measure his length in the dust, out cold.

It took the other two troopers, both as shocked as Grimble, a few moments to convince themselves that this feisty old lady was a force to be reckoned with, and those few moments cost them dearly; they recoiled as she dashed at them and, by then, it was too late. She swung upward. The end of her club connected with a chin and the owner thereof was well and truly unconscious before he went down shoulders-first.

The third soldier was intimidated when Hattie advanced on him. Understandably so, what with one of his buddies in a state of oblivion on the sidewalk and the other sprawled in the street in a similar condition. He opted for a strategic retreat, turned and fled northward along the sidewalk, but not a great distance; Hattie wasn't through with him.

Grimble's jaw sagged and pedestrians hastily vacated the area. Hattie had a clear, if running, target, as she twirled and hurled the pickaxe handle. And her accuracy was deadly. The missile flew low, wedging between two fast-moving legs with the inevitable result. The trooper nose-dived, hitting the sidewalk with such impact that a dry plank snapped.

'I believe he too is immobilized,' murmured the "old lady", turning to the stunned Grimble. 'And now, young man, having witnessed this disgraceful incident, I suggest it is your duty to report it to Major Royle.'

Reluctant to disagree with the aged woman who had just rendered three men senseless, Grimble doffed his hat and mumbled,

'Yes, ma'am.'

'The major must be made to realize that the men under his command are behaving in a most ungallant manner toward the ladies of Shayville – this time a mere schoolgirl.'

'Yes, ma'am.'

'I strongly advise you to obtain help and remove those ruffians to their quarters.'

'Yes, ma'am.'

'Thank you.'

While onlookers gawked, 'Mrs Elmira Tebbutt' quit the scene with head held high. A few overawed locals applauded; this she acknowledged with a gracious nod.

Recovering his composure, Grimble beckoned

acquaintances.

'Henry, Leroy, lend a hand here. We're takin' these heroes to the Grand.'

The arrival of the deputy and his helpers, hauling three troopers much the worse for wear, won a startled and hostile reaction from other troopers and a noncom. Grimble and his friends dumped their burdens by the reception desk. Gruffly, he announced.

'They got outa line and got what they deserved – from just one old lady. I saw the whole thing and I ain't here to argue about it.'

'Listen, you …!' began the corporal.

'One of 'em was pawin' a kid just outa school,' scowled Grimble. 'Just how low can you soldier-boys get? Shayville folks ain't takin' no more of such devilry. Tell *that* to the major.'

It was a tense moment. A pitched brawl might have erupted but for the presence of Lieutenant Purvis; he had descended the stairs in time to overhear the deputy's statement. Sighting him, the noncom restrained the would-be aggressors.

'Ten-*hun!*'

All but the unconscious soldiers stood to attention.

'At ease,' ordered Purvis, moving away from the stairs. 'But stand by – quietly.' He nodded to Grimble. 'If you please, Deputy, a fuller explanation.'

Grimble offered a more detailed account of the hullabaloo in his own rough, ungrammatical way; Purvis winced while listening, the deputy's English being as distressing to his ears as the incident he was reporting.

'The – uh – so aggressive lady was, I presume, Mrs Tebbutt?'

'Who else?' grinned Grimble.

'Thank you, Deputy,' nodded Purvis. 'You may leave it to me to relay your report to my superior. Corporal, I'm sure you've anticipated my next order. Arrange for transfer of these men to ...'

'A doc,' scowled the corporal. '*More* business for a local sawbones.'

'At once,' urged Purvis.

His polite gesture was an invitation for the deputy and his friends to depart. They did so, after which the lieutenant returned to the stairs and climbed to the top floor. Soon afterward, he was dropping this latest bombshell on Major Royle, not from a great height, but with devastating impact.

Red-faced, beside himself with indignation, Royle declared,

'An outrage! This is the last straw!'

'I'm sure that's exactly how the citizens of Shayville feel, sir,' said Purvis. 'About everything.'

'I've tried to be reasonable!' blustered Royle. 'To appease that harridan, I gave permission for a resumption of her – her self-defence classes – and this is how she repays me!'

'My apologies, Major, if I did not express myself clearly. The incident involved a trooper making overtures to a schoolgirl. The child was terrified, Deputy Grimble remonstrated, Mrs Tebbutt happened to be in the vicinity ...'

'Lieutenant, I heard you the first time!'

'Yes, sir. Justified indignation, you must agree. After all, there are limits.'

'There are limits, Lieutenant, to my patience!'

'Of course. I do realize these are troublesome times for you.'

'No trouble I can't handle, damn it! I'm the most competent officer of the Third Cavalry, and don't you forget it. I thrive on trouble. I welcome every challenge.'

'Sir, you are an inspiration to us all.'

Royle grimaced uneasily. Less pomade and easy on the moustache wax, Purvis was thinking. The major was sweating again. With the usual effect.

'Hell, Purvis.' He grimaced again and shook his head. 'This can't go on.'

'I agree,' nodded Purvis. 'But, begging the major's pardon, I have, with all due respect, attempted to sound a note of caution. Civilians will only endure so much, and this is not the first time our men have behaved – how should I put this? Impulsively, with no thought for the consequences of their actions?'

'Confound it,' sighed Royle. 'I face the prospect of schooling my men in the social graces – which is ridiculous!'

That night, in a back room of a downtown saloon, six conspirators were in conference, speaking softly, their voices barely rising above a whisper. The leader of the group was reminded.

'It's that time.'

'Think I've forgotten?' was the gruff reply. 'Tomorrow's the day. We move out a couple hours before sunrise. How about the rig?'

'It'll be ready.'

'Then we're all set. All we gotta do is dig up the merchandise, load it and deliver it. By noon, we'll be tradin' it for a fortune in gold.'

'I guess – uh – Bearcat'll deal square.'

'Bet your ass he'll deal square. He *wants* that Gatlin' – bad.'

'So, he gets what he wants, we get what we want.'

'Nobody's told me yet. How do we find where

Bearcat's camped? He knows we're fetchin' it by wagon, but there won't be no wagon route through the Laberinto Hills.'

The man who had planned and executed the hijacking of the Gatling gun grinned at the curious one and assured him,

'We won't have to search for the hideaway. Bearcat promised me he'd post a scout. The scout'll be waitin' for us. He'll guide us to the hideout, Crane. And you just know there'll be some kinda route. Might be rough, not a regular trail, but it'll get us there.'

Another man made a prediction.

'Gonna be hell to pay in this territory when that renegade gets his hands on the Gatling. I wonder what he'll attack first. This town – or Camp Kemp?'

'No skin off of our noses.' The boss-conspirator chuckled callously. 'We'll've disappeared by the time he starts raisin' hell. Kansas-bound we'll be. We divide all them nuggets six ways and we'll be rich enough to live high off the hog the rest of our lives.'

'Sometimes I wonder about tearaways like Bearcat – Quanah Parker too,' mused the man seated beside him. 'Half-breeds with a big hate for whites. What's in it for 'em? They can't hold out forever. Not Cochise, not Geronimo, not any of 'em. They think they'll never be stopped? Hell, they must be crazy.'

'Bearcat's crazy like a fox,' opined another man. 'Keeps outsmartin' the army. Sure, he'll get his sooner or later. But, meanwhile, he'll be havin' himself a killin' spree.'

Their leader decided.

'Best we get some shut-eye while we can. Gotta remember we're makin' an early start.'

In the wee small hours of the following morning, the

six rogues made a quiet exit from the big town – their last exit – and made for the flats away to the east, two on the wagon-seat, the other four riding escort and leading two saddled horses.

Rick was, at this time, taking his turn at sitting watch at the east rim of the timber, his gaze turned westward. Still in his Julius Fairchild role, he was mentally speculating on the outcome of his strategy. Not many doubts in his mind. He had, he assured himself, made deductions and formed hunches, all of which made sense.

If he had figured it wrong, the next riders he and his companeros sighted would approach from the south, the Laberinto Hills, some of Bearcat Webster's braves coming to retrieve the Gatling. Still a lot of questions to which he had no answers. Why cache the gun at all? Why leave it here so long?

The other possibility was taking shape in his mind when Sheriff Strother, shrouded in a poncho, joined him. The lawman squatted and muttered.

'I'm takin' over from you, Chuck. Go get some sleep.'

'In a little while, Vin my friend,' said Rick. 'Not sleepy right now. Too much on my mind.'

'We should be thankful we aren't doing this in mid-winter,' drawled Strother. 'Freeze our butts way out here. There'd be snow. We couldn't survive without a fire. Too much on your mind, huh? Careful, old timer. You could get brain-weary.'

'It doesn't work that way with me. Rumination keeps my brain well-oiled.'

'Lucky you. I get plumb tuckered out trying to figure how Shayville folks're ever gonna get rid of Royle's Roughnecks.'

'I've told you how, Vin. Trust me.'

'Trust you like I'd trust a brother. Still seems too much to hope for though, delivering the Gatling to Colonel Cobcroft along with the polecats who hijacked it, making him admit Shayville needs no garrison force, no martial law.'

'Don't forget our edge. We've found the Gatling. I call that a good start.'

'It sure helps, but it doesn't win us anything unless somebody comes to dig it up.'

'That has to happen. To steal it, cache it and *leave* it defies logic. Somebody'll show, Vin. Count on it.'

'Well, I'm wondering how long a wait this'll be.'

'Have faith in my instincts.'

'Got a gut-feeling, huh?'

'Very strong, Vin, very strong. And it tells me our vigil will soon end.'

Rick rose, patted Strother's shoulder and withdrew to the clearing.

It was nearing sunrise when he came awake, roused by the stirring of Roy Bass, Bruno Hyatt and Jerry Kilburn; Strother had called to them. Hefting their weapons, they quit the clearing to join the sheriff, who was staring not north nor south, but west.

'That spyglass of yours, Jerry,' he said tensely. 'Loan it to Chuck – so he'll see 'em clearer – so I'll know my eyes aren't playing wild tricks on me.'

Rick accepted the telescope, raised it and focussed on the distant, slowing approaching vehicle and riders. Despite the pre-dawn gloom, he could distinguish more clearly what Strother had seen in silhouette.

'What …?' began the deputy.

'Am I wrong or are they troopers?' Strother demanded of Rick.

'We'll know for sure by the time they reach the

rocks,' said Rick, returning the telescope. 'Full light by then. Meanwhile, I'm going down there. I want to be concealed, ready to observe and listen – a little eavesdropping – from this side of one of those big boulders.'

'Not by yourself you ain't,' growled the blacksmith.

'All right,' said Rick. 'Vin, you, Bruno and me. Roy and Jerry stay hidden here. This could be vital, this spying expedition. It's important we don't reveal ourselves before we hear some talk. If we challenged them the moment they arrived, we'd be fed a pack of lies. It would be their word against ours. Does everybody understand?'

'Old timer, you make a lot of sense,' approved Kilburn.

'So,' grinned Rick. 'Let's do it.'

Tagged by Strother and Hyatt, he broke from the timber. They descended toward the rocks bent low and reached vantage-points a few minutes before the sun began rising beyond the county seat. Rick was sharing a rock with the sheriff, Hyatt's bulk concealed behind the one to their left. He edged half of his face around his hiding place to briefly study the approaching rig.

'Troopers?' frowned Strother.

'But not from Camp Kemp,' muttered Rick, crouching again. 'Not unless they travelled a wide half-circle before heading this way. More likely – in fact I'm certain – they're six of the Shayville garrison force.'

'What makes you so sure?' challenged Hyatt.

'I recognized the driver,' said Rick. 'We've met, but not socially. He's the noncom whose nose I damaged at the Glad Hand Saloon.'

'The sergeant – Hake?' scowled Strother.

'In the unappealing flesh,' nodded Rick. 'My friends, this is going to be interesting. Remember now, we keep our heads down and our ears cocked till I decide we should reveal ourselves.'

'Savvy, Bruno?' prodded Strother.

'Hey, I can be patient – if I try,' Hyatt assured him.

'Word hard at it,' urged Strother.

'But I wanta know somethin' here and now,' said Hyatt. 'Are we gonna let 'em dig that devil gun up?'

'Bruno, we'll even let them load it onto the rig,' shrugged Rick. 'And why not? Let *them* handle all the hard toil, while we conserve our energy. They aren't taking it anywhere – but I want to know where they *intended* taking it.'

'Chuck's right again,' said Strother. 'You got it, Bruno? We're gonna listen to learn.'

'Sounds good to me,' mumbled the blacksmith. 'I'm as curious as you two.'

With boulders at the east part of the semi-circle concealing them from view of the oncoming troopers, they waited and listened. Hake hauled back on his reins, stalling the open wagon by the division on the west side.

Before descending, he rose to scan the surrounding terrain.

'All clear,' he announced. 'Okay now, out with the tools and let's get to diggin'. We got an appointment, real important business.' He guffawed as he dropped to the ground. 'And it ain't polite to keep 'em waitin' – them we got business with.'

Rick and the sheriff traded glances. Strother's eyes were gleaming. They listened to the sounds of activity, spades and pickaxes and shovels clattering as they were taken from the wagonbed, then the thudding as the digging operation began, the spading of loosened earth and Hake's mumbled insistence that the diggers work with care.

'Workin' as careful as we can, Gunther,' panted a trooper.

'Can't take no chances,' warned Hake. 'You cut the tarp or the inside coverin', you'll let a lotta dirt in. First thing Bearcat'll wanta do is test it. If it's all clogged up, he'll turn mean. Don't forget his whole war party'll be with him. C'mon, hustle, but do it careful.'

Hyatt's eyebrows shot up. He stared across at Rick and the sheriff. Strother was scowling in fury, Rick impassive.

More instructions from Hake when the digging ceased. His accomplices were urged to raise the weapon slowly. Rick and his companions heard much grunting and gasping, followed by Hake's reaction after raising a flap of the tarp. Plainly, he hadn't spotted the tear made by Rick's knife.

'Looks fine, yeah, right. Now we load it. You, Mitch, fetch them magazines along, all the ammo.'

When Rick raised his head, the backs of the six were turned to him. He watched the Gatling loaded onto the wagon, then nodded to Strother and Hyatt.

'That's it,' said Hake. 'Mount up and let's get goin'.'

Before he could clamber aboard the rig, before any of the others could raise boots to stirrups, Rick called to them and broke cover, accompanied by Strother and the blacksmith. The excavation had been filled in, but they stepped clear of the soft patch.

'No!' countered Rick. 'Stay just as you are!'

Strother whistled. Bass and Kilburn promptly broke from the trees and came on at the double, both brandishing rifles. For a long moment, six rogues in uniform were shocked immobile, gaping at the three men advancing on them. Hake was first to rally. The flap of his cavalry issue holster was folded back to permit a fast cross draw of his pistol. He was beginning his draw when Rick whisked his Colt from leather and leapt at him, swinging. The barrel made hard contact with the side of Hake's head. Hake flopped unconscious.

In panic, a trooper began mounting his horse. Big Bruno reached him fast and, one-handed, separated him from the animal and swung him against a rock. Strother's rifle was covering the others, as were the weapons held by his deputy and the gunsmith.

Bass was irate.

'We oughta gun 'em down right now!' he raged.

'That would be too merciful, Roy,' said Rick. Unnoticed by the rogue soldiers, he alerted with a sly wink the grim-faced Strother. 'I have other plans for them. Any objections, Vin?'

'You're bossin' this deal,' shrugged Strother.

The soldiers, conscious and otherwise, were disarmed and, with their horses, taken up the slant to the timber and into the clearing. The wagon and its two-horse team weren't moved. Finding rope in the vehicle, Bass fetched it along.

Kilburn gave vent to his outrage, backhanding a trooper so savagely that he cringed and flopped on his backside.

'Sons of bitches!' fumed the gunsmith.

'Gentlemen,' said Rick. 'We begin by securing the prisoners.'

Strother and Bass unhitched their manacles. With the rope, with belts, the six captives were secured hand and foot and dumped in a row. It was time for Rick to give a performance, and he played his role convincingly, dropping to one knee beside an apprehensive trooper, unholstering his Colt again and pressing the muzzle to his sweating brow.

'A great deal more needs explaining, Vin,' he said calmly. 'I believe at least one of these traitors will answer my questions. If he's reluctant to co-operate, he's of no use to us. I'll execute him and interrogate the next man.'

'You can't let him!' cried the trooper, staring up at Strother. 'Hell, you're a lawman!'

Strother made a small ceremony of unfastening and pocketing his star; Bass followed suit.

'A credit to the U.S. Cavalry you are, I don't think,' scowled Strother. 'I can't get my mind off that Gatling – what Bearcat Webster'd do with it, all the people he'd butcher. You and these other skunks aimed to hand it over to him, so how much mercy do you figure you deserve?'

'Let's start with your name,' said Rick. The trooper blinked at him. He pressed harder with his Colt and thumbed back the hammer. The trooper's eyes bulged. 'Immediate answers, brave soldier – or else!'

'Crane!' gasped the trooper. 'George Crane.'

'Tell 'em nothin', Crane!' one of his cronies urged.

Without shifting his gaze, Rick enquired of that one,

'Will you say nothing – when I reach you? You're third in line. By the time I'm ready for you, Crane and another hero will have proved to you – the hard way – that I mean business.'

'George, it's our necks!' another man warned.

'Shuddup!' Hyatt snarled at him.

'You will now tell us about the theft of the Gatling from the armoury,' commanded Rick, baring his teeth.

Crane shuddered and closed his eyes.

'That was Gunther – and Mitch and Corey. They – wore moccasins ...'

'And murdered the quartermaster sergeant and the trooper on guard.'

'It was Gunther ...'

'Sergeant Hake.'

'Yeah, him. He never liked Smitty and Cleland anyway.'

'Why cache the Gatling?'

'Gunther needed time to – uh-to set things up with Bearcat – work out a deal, a trade. Him and Bearcat know each other – got acquainted – I dunno how.'

'I'll make a guess,' said Rick. 'It was Bearcat and some of his braves massacred the prospectors at the Lucky Seven claim. Hake's agreement with Bearcat – the Gatling for the gold?'

'It's all raw nuggets – sacks of it – the pure stuff.'

'You are staying alive by talking. Tell us more. And – a warning – no lies. You lie. I'll know. And that'll be the death of you.'

'Better believe it, Crane,' advised Bass. 'Old Chuck can read a man's mind.'

'You'd have taken the Gatling to Bearcat – when?' asked Rick.

Hake had regained consciousness. Struggling against his bonds, he stared about wildly. Profanity spilled from his contorted mouth. And then his gaze fastened on the terrified Crane and the apparently old but so formidable man threatening him.

'What the hell ...?' he cried.

'You blind?' challenged Crane. 'What d'you think he's pokin' at me – a cigar?'

Bass couldn't restrain his curiosity. Rick was eager to continue the interrogation, but gave the deputy some leeway.

'Somethin' I still don't savvy,' Bass protested. 'Why'd Hake stash the Gatlin' *here*?'

'Crane, when I get my hands on you …!' gasped Hake.

'One more word out of you and, so help me, I'll gutshoot you – Sergeant!' breathed Strother. 'Of all the stinkin' traitors, of all the lowdown hypocrites …!'

'Patience, Vin my friend,' Rick said gently. 'Crane is about to satisfy Roy's curiosity.'

'He had to plant the gun here,' muttered Crane. 'The storm. Nobody counted on the storm. This was as far as they could haul it.'

'I'll now repeat my last question,' said Rick. 'The delivery to Bearcat?'

Crane was a broken man. He would have told them anything now, his date of birth, date of enlistment, how many teeth he had, the last time he washed his underwear – anything.

'Today,' he sighed. 'We were to move on from here, all the way to the Laberintos – and Bearcat's hideout.'

'Nobody knows the hideout,' argued Strother. 'Only that damn renegade and his killer-bunch.'

'Bearcat'll have a scout posted, waitin' for us,' said Crane. 'The scout – he'll guide us to the camp. I mean – he would've.'

Rick smiled, straightened up and uncocked and reholstered his Colt.

'That's it?' frowned Kilburn.

'We know all we need to know,' said Rick. 'You all heard Trooper Crane's statement. Two law officers and three civilians. I'm sure Colonel Cobcroft will believe what we have to tell him – however reluctantly.'

'By damn, we've done it!' grinned Bass.

'Hey, I can't wait to see the look on the colonel's

kisser,' chuckled Big Bruno, 'when we show up at Camp Kemp with these skunks – and the Gatlin'.'

'Proud day for me,' declared Strother. 'Eyeball to eyeball with Cobcroft, flashin' my badge, challengin' him. Oh, sure, that'll pleasure me, and then some. "Colonel," I'm gonna say, "what the hell does Shayville need with martial law, if civilians can fetch the Gatlin' back to you, along with a half-dozen rogues under your command, includin' your brave sergeant that butchered two of your men?" Damn right, Bruno. I'm with you. Can't wait to see the look on his face.'

While his companions gloated, anticipating Camp Kemp's reaction to the recovery of the Gatling and the apprehension by civilians of six of their comrades who'd gone bad, Rick lit a cigar, turned his back and retreated to the west side of the clearing to stare away to the rocks, the wagon and its deadly cargo, the horses in harness. Another idea was forming in his mind. Big, Audacious. Outlandish maybe. But oh so logical. It could work, he assured himself. There would be risks, but it could work.

His allies were in high spirits now, calling to him jubilantly.

'What d'you say, Chuck?'

'What're we waitin' for?'

'Time to get goin', old feller. Camp Kemp next stop.'

He rejoined them, seated himself and eyed them one by one, the blacksmith, the gunsmith, the elated Bass, then Strother. It was an exciting moment for him, but he managed to stay in character, to address Strother as a much older man, the oldest man present.

'Vin, there's so much more we could achieve this day,' he said. 'One thing I've endeavoured to avoid throughout my long career, my early years as a scout and Indian fighter is – un-finished business, work only half-completed. Yes, Vin, I hate to do things by halves.'

Hyatt, Bass and the gunsmith traded puzzled looks.

'What're you gettin' at, Chuck?' demanded Strother.

'It would be impressive, a severe blow to the regiment, our returning the Gatling to Camp Kemp with the rogues who hijacked it and their accomplices,' said Rick. 'But, my dear friends ...' He addressed all four of them now, 'we'd make an even greater impact, prove decisively that the Shayville bankers who petitioned for martial law are just muddle-headed pantywaists ...'

'If ...?' prodded Strother.

'If we brought them all in,' said Rick. 'Not just these rogue-soldiers. Bearcat Webster and his whole band. And, for good measure – I don't like loose ends – the gold looted from the Lucky Seven claim.'

Hake, fearful Strother would make good on his threat, didn't dare speak. Neither did his cronies. But they were taken aback. As for the lawmen, the blacksmith and the gunsmith, they were incredulous.

Kilburn said soothingly,

'Old man, you've figured everything right – up till now. This deal worked out just like you set it up. We admire you for that. But – no offence – you're talking wild now.'

'Chuck, I'll admit I'm feelin' greedy,' said Strother. 'But – Bearcat and all his bucks? Only five of us. Maybe you're forgettin' that. Five, Chuck. Against that whole bunch of ...?'

'Bearcat's waiting for the Gatling,' Rick said casually. '*We* have the Gatling, plus the ammunition for it. It's operational and I've no doubt, with a little help from Jerry, I could get the knack of using it. And we have another ace in the hole. Uniforms. Bearcat's scout will be on the lookout for the wagon and an escort of cavalrymen who've betrayed their regiment. We can do it, Vin. The scout will lead us to Bearcat's hideout – and the gold – and, though heavily outnumbered, we'll have the edge.'

'Meanin' the devil gun!' Hyatt said hoarsely. 'Lawd Almighty!'

'Hell's bells!' breathed Kilburn.

Bass asked hesitantly.

'It could work? We could really do it?'

'Being outnumbered sounds intimidating,' Rick conceded. 'But how are those renegades armed?'

'Rifles – and I don't mean single-shot muskets,' said Strother. 'Few pistols maybe. Warbows, lances, tomahawks for sure.'

'By the time they try attacking us, I could demoralize them,' Rick assured him. 'A few bursts from the Gatling, Vin. I believe we'd make our point, convince them to surrender. It's a fearsome weapon.'

'Throws fifty calibre rounds – and fast,' muttered Kilburn.

'Gentlemen, I would not propose such a strategy were I not certain we'd succeed,' declared Rick.

'Go on,' invited Strother. 'We're still listenin'.'

'I'll be in the wagon with the gun, concealed under the tarp,' said Rick. 'You and the others – except for the man driving the wagon – will be riding army horses. I won't reveal myself till we reach Bearcat's lair. If he and his braves offer resistance – can you doubt our ability to discourage them?'

Bass's eyes gleamed.

'Vin,' he said. 'You decide.'

# 7

# Five for the Showdown

In broad daylight, Sheriff Strother's dreams had to be daydreams, daydreams of glory. His hesitation lasted but a few moments, because he had a mind-picture of it all, the possibilities, the probabilities, the golden opportunity he had craved since martial law began.

'We're gonna do it,' he announced.

'We certainly are, my friend,' grinned Rick. 'And now, a few essentials. Who's the best wagon driver we have?'

'Me,' the blacksmith promptly insisted. ''Sides, I just volunteered.'

'You'd be a good choice anyway, Bruno,' approved Rick. 'You're of a size with Hake, his uniform should fit you and he probably intended driving anyway. Let's get busy, my brave comrades. Our prisoners have to be untied and stripped – one by one. Each of you will change to a uniform. We'll then resecure them and, for good measure, gag and blindfold them. We leave our horses here and take four of theirs.'

'Collect 'em later, huh?' guessed Bass.

'For sure, Roy,' nodded Rick. 'The civilian law officers of Shay County will this day present the

Third Cavalry with quite a prize, a mixed bag. Let's get to it.'

Crane was first to be untied and stripped of his uniform. Kilburn held the tunic against himself and eyed his friends inquiringly. They nodded and, a few minutes later, he was rigged as a trooper and Crane rebound, gagged and blindfolded.

The process was repeated with the now frightened Hake and, watching the blacksmith donning the sergeant's uniform, Rick noted a facial resemblance. Hyatt was not a complete lookalike; too much to expect. But, with Hake's hat pulled low over his brow, he could pass scrutiny.

Soon enough, Strother and his deputy were in uniform, all six captives bound so tightly that their chances of escape were minimal and all weapons, civilian and army issue, collected; at Rick's insistence, every prisoner was searched for a concealed knife.

They quit the clearing and made for the rocks and the wagon, Strother, his deputy and the gunsmith straddling cavalry mounts, Rick and Hyatt on foot.

The blacksmith climbed to the seat. Rick clambered in back, pulled the tarp away, then the oilskin. Kilburn nudged his horse close and offered advice. A magazine was fitted into position. Rick took control of the Gatling, swinging its revolving barrels toward the timber, then upward. He gripped the firing handle.

'Turn it as though working a mangle?'

'That's how,' nodded Kilburn. 'Ring poking up, that's your sight, and you turn that handle fast as you want to throw those big bullets.'

'A few rounds, just for practice,' Rick decided.

On its tripod, the well-lubricated weapon moved easily. He aimed for the treetops from a half-kneeling position and gave the handle two complete turns. The

Gatling chug-chugged ominously and, before the eyes of the watching men, high branches were cut loose and foliage scattered. He hoped the branches would topple into the clearing; well, they had to fall *somewhere*.

'Great day in the mornin'!' gasped Bass.

'Bruno, when we reach our destination, turn this vehicle,' instructed Rick. 'A full circle. Better – if necessary – I direct fire over the tailgate. That, I believe, would be preferable to firing over the team's heads.'

'I'll remember, old feller,' promised Hyatt.

'All right, Chuck, hide yourself under that tarp,' urged Strother. 'And let's roll.'

'Heeyaaah ...!' Hyatt yelled to the team.

The vehicle started southward at steady speed, the riders keeping pace, their eyes on the hazy rises of the Laberinto Hills.

For a mile and a half, silence, the men wrapped in their own thoughts. Probably, Rick supposed, estimating their chances of surviving this desperate enterprise. Prolonged abstinence from conversation tended to irritate Big Bruno. He had to say something – anything.

'Well,' he cheerily remarked. 'We got us a right fine day for it.'

'That's a fact,' agreed Bass. 'Right fine day.'

With a heavy touch of bravado, Kilburn growled.

'Any day's a good day for settlin' that half-breed's hash. No-good, kill-crazy son of a bitch.'

'Cavalry never could plan how to get to him,' said Strother. 'But we sure did. Well – Chuck did. How're you doin' under there, Chuck?'

'A tad too warm for comfort, but no complaints,' came Rick's muffled reply. 'All in a good cause after all.'

'Sure you can handle this kinda action?' Hyatt asked over his shoulder. 'You move real slick for a feller so old, but you must be tirin'.'

'What d'you say, Chuck?' called Bass.

'Mind over matter,' Rick said reassuringly. 'I pace myself. Right now, I'm resting, conserving my energy. When required to perform, I'll be rejuvenated, ready for anything. You young fellows shouldn't worry about me. Stay alert, concentrate on your own welfare.'

'Suppose the scout parleys English?' frowned Kilburn.

'We'll know when he hails us – *if* he hails us,' said Rick. 'It's just as likely he'll do no more than signal us. Then, Bruno, you follow him.'

'No trail through those damn hills, not that anybody knows of,' declared Strother.

'There'll be some kinda route,' opined Hyatt. 'Like the trooper said, Bearcat's waitin' for us and knows we're haulin' that devil gun in a rig.'

Two more miles. They were drawing closer to the hills.

'About time we decided how we're gonna handle this,' said Strother. 'What d'you say, Chuck?'

'I'm appointing you spokesman,' said Rick. 'Bruno should not speak. We have to remember Hake was his contact, so he's familiar with the sergeant's voice. Did I say sergeant? Make that ex-sergeant.'

'Damn right,' Bass said grimly. 'A noncom and a trooper butchered means ...'

'A courtmartial and a hangrope,' said Strother. 'Keep talkin', Chuck.'

'They'll all be hungering for their glimpse of the Gatling.' Rick called this a safe prediction. 'After Bruno turns the wagon, you'll lower the tailgate and uncover the gun, making sure the tarp's still covering me. Then – and be firm about this – you'll demand to be shown the gold. No trading till you see it. We don't want to waste time searching for wherever they've cached it.'

'After that?' asked Strother.

'I'll make my entrance,' said Rick.

'Do what?' blinked Hyatt.

'Sorry. Just an expression,' Rick apologized. 'I meant to say I'll reveal myself and demand their surrender. If I back my demand by demonstrating just what this Gatling can do, send enough bullets to kick up a straight line of dust ...'

'That'll scare the gizzards outa 'em,' guffawed Hyatt.

'Yes, the demonstration may well have the desired effect,' said Rick.

'They'll quit cold?' challenged Kilburn. 'I don't know, Chuck. Might be too much to hope for.'

'We'll find out – either way,' said Strother, staring ahead. 'Better we don't talk no more, boys. The lookout's spotted us by now. Just keep goin' – Sergeant Hyatt.'

'Call me that again, Vin Strother,' scowled the blacksmith, 'and I'll stuff your tin star right down your damn gullet.'

The vehicle and escorts were twenty yards from the base of the first slope when Strother sighted the lookout. Mounted and hefting a lance, the Arapaho emerged from brush above and to their right and signalled the party. Hyatt turned the team and the first ascent began.

Staying some fifteen yards ahead, the scout led them onward through terrain the vehicle could travel, but only just. The Laberintos were well-named. Their progress wound through draws, around the bases of rises, up and down slopes and skirted clumps of timber the variety of which was bewildering. Firs and spruce here and there, broad leaf hardwoods along with limbers and quaking aspens.

Nobody tried to memorize the route. No need. Wheel-ruts would be their guide during the return journey – if there was to be a return journey.

Finally they reached it, the mouth of a not too big canyon which, when they followed their guide into it, proved to be a box. Deputy Bass at once began counting the tied horses away to their left, almost thirty, he figured. The guide rode on to join braves emerging from tepees, a motley bunch, all of them armed. Hard against the canyon's blind end Strother noted a mound of dry branches.

At a muttered command from the sheriff, Hyatt turned the team in a circle and stalled the wagon with its rear end facing the tepees and the redmen. From his lodge some distance from the tepees, a tall man emerged to raise a hand in greeting.

'Has to be Bearcat,' Strother muttered to Rick as he lowered the tailgate.

Bass was reflecting that Bearcat Webster was bad medicine on two legs. Hyatt felt the same way. Kilburn, sitting his horse close by the wagon, managed to stay impassive, masking his anger and animosity.

The chief of these rebellious Arapahos stood six feet two inches tall in his moccasined feet. His headgear was a sombrero set at a rakish angle atop the mane of coal-black, shoulder-length hair. The face was high cheekboned, the complexion light, proving he had been sired by a white man. The cold blue eyes were also a dead giveaway. It was not a handsome visage. A scar ran from left ear, downward then straight across the chin. He was naked from the waist up, except for an amulet. His pants were fringed buckskin. He carried a lance. And a great deal of muscle.

'You show the gold, we show the big gun,' Strother called to him. 'Straight trade, Chief. You savvy English, so you know what I'm sayin'.'

Bearcat Webster came to a halt, lips parting to reveal yellowing teeth.

'Savvy English good,' he growled at Strother. 'I hear what you say and I understand. Now *you* hear *me* and understand. Show the gun – *now*.'

Strother nodded to Kilburn, who leaned from his saddle to grasp the front end of the canvas and fold it back, revealing the Gatling, still concealing Rick. Unholy glee showed in Webster's eyes. He half-turned to jabber at his warriors. Three of them promptly hurried to the mound against the rear rock wall and began removing dry branches.

It took them only a minute or two to uncover what six prospectors had been massacred for, and one maimed for life. Strother stared hard at the sacks of soft leather, each slightly smaller than a two-pound floursack, the necks secured by rawhide.

'Okay,' he said just loud enough for Rick to hear. 'We can see the gold. If we're ever gonna do it – now's the time.'

Rick swiftly rid himself of the tarp and assumed his firing position behind the Gatling. Webster tensed, glaring at him.

'The name is Fairchild, Mister Webster,' Rick called to him. 'You hungered for this weapon because you admire its fire-power. I will prove how deadly it is – unless you at once order your men to disarm themselves and surrender to us!'

For a moment, Webster appeared dumbfounded. Rick could understand why, having challenged him in his quavery old man voice. Still using that mode of speech, and drawing on his knowledge of the Arapaho dialect, he repeated his challenge with the Gatling turned toward the gaping braves.

One of them loosed a war-whoop and drew back his arm to hurl a lance. He froze in that posture as Rick cut loose, turning the firing handle, sending heavy calibre slugs slamming into the ground in a straight line some two yards this side of a row of moccasined feet. The effect on the redmen was instant; they recoiled, bug-eyed.

Something snapped in Webster's mind. He yelled in fury.

'They are only five! Kill – kill – *kill* …!'

Another burst from the Gatling. The intimidated braves did not drop their weapons, but retreated several paces. Webster then called Rick several names at the top of his voice, including son of a bitch and paleface bastard.

'Jerry, take over from me,' Rick sharply ordered.

He waited for the gunsmith to part company with his saddle and flop, then started Strother frantically protesting by making for the tailgate the moment Kilburn was manning the Gatling.

'Don't tangle with him, Chuck! He's too strong for you! You can't …!'

'He's mine!' insisted Rick, and dropped to the ground.

As Webster made to hurl his lance, Roy Bass emptied his holster and made everybody, the redskins included, acknowledge he was a mean hand with a Colt. The weapon boomed. The bullet hit the shaft of the lance three inches from where Webster was grasping it, neatly severing it. Webster cursed, flung the remaining half away and unsheathed a knife. He charged at Rick, who neither backstepped nor sidestepped, but bounded forward.

The impact was savage, but he achieved his purpose, his left hand clamping tight as a vice about the wrist of the hand gripping the knife. They reeled as they grappled. He was fighting for his life, concentrating on pitting his strength against that of a maniacal killer but, even in this harrowing situation, hoping his wig and false face whiskers would stay with him.

As they lurched back and forth, their every move was followed by Strother and his deputy, both with guns drawn. Hyatt with his cocked shotgun and Kilburn with the Gatling covering the redmen didn't dare shift their eyes.

With his free hand, Webster clawed for Rick's eyes. Rick discouraged him by biting into a finger. The half-breed screamed and withdrew the hand. With his own bunched right, Rick pounded the naked torso. He was maintaining pressure with his left hand, forcing the blade away from his own body when his adversary hooked a leg about his and threw all his weight against him.

He couldn't maintain his balance. As he began falling, he twisted harder. And then he was down with Webster atop him, his whole scarred face contorted, the blue eyes bulging. He turned his head in time to see Strother levelling his Colt.

'Don't!' he called.

'I can put one in his head without hittin' you!' cried Strother. 'Don't worry, Chuck! I got a clear bead!'

'No – need …!' panted Rick.

He planted his hands against the naked shoulders,

shoved hard to start Webster rolling, then rolled out
from under him. Bearcat Webster now sprawled on
his back, only the hilt of the knife showing, the whole
blade embedded in his chest by the impact of their
fall, blood spattering from either side of the mortal
wound.

The moaning of the renegades was a gut-chilling
sound. They stared aghast at the ultimate morale-
breaker, their lifeless leader, their inspiration,
sprawled there, the loser of a fight to the death with a
paleface who looked to be double his age. As Rick
retrieved his hat and came upright, back turned to his
allies and the Arapahos while he worriedly checked
his disguise, the death chanting began. For Bearcat
Webster's followers, his death was the ultimate
demoralizer.

But Kilburn was taking no chances, covering them,
working the Gatling's barrels from side to side.

'Hell's sakes, Chuck, you're too damn foolhardy for
your own good!' chided Strother.

'This seemed the best way, Vin,' Rick replied.
'Break their morale, you save a lot of bloodshed. With
their leader dead and the Gatling scaring hell out of
'em, I believe they can be convinced they're all
through.'

'You know enough of their lingo to convince 'em?'
challenged the blacksmith.

'Only one way to find out,' said Rick.

Standing beside Webster's body, clear of the line of
fire, he made his speech. After his first few words, the
chanting died down; he had an attentive audience.
He began by pointing sternly to the body, then to the
Gatling. Their chief was en route to the Happy
Hunting Grounds and, if he, the slayer of their chief,
gave the command, the devil gun would speak again.

In only a few moments, they would be as dead as Bearcat.

'Think you're getting it across to 'em?' asked Bass.

'Roy, I'm doing my damnedest,' Rick assured him, and continued.

The dejected redmen were warned their rampaging days were over. From this place, they would ride under guard, menaced by the devil gun every mile of their journey all the way to the headquarters of the long knives. Only by disarming themselves, surrendering here and now and obeying orders from here on, could they hope to survive. The Great White Father, as represented by Colonel Cobcroft of the 3rd Cavalry, would decide their fate. With them they would bring the gold looted from the white prospectors. The traitor long knife who had conspired with Bearcat had been captured. They had nothing to gain, but something to lose, namely their lives. They would decide now. If one of them raised a weapon, they would be slaughtered. With their own eyes, they had seen what the devil gun could do – to all of them.

'I don't think they'll take long to decide,' he told Strother, while the Indians mumbled among themselves. 'Keep your hardware ready for action, and Jerry, a ferocious look if you please. They have to believe you mean business.'

'Am I smiling, looking friendly?' retorted the gunsmith. 'Listen, old man, I'm in a mood to cut down the whole lousy pack!'

The parley was over; the redmen began discarding rifles, lances, tomahawks, knives, warbows and quivers of arrows, all their weapons. During this, Strother came to where Rick stood.

'I'm still tryin' to believe it,' he confided. 'By glory, Chuck, we did it! Or better I should say *you* did it.'

'Alone and unaided?' said Rick. 'Come, my friend, you know better than that. Spread the credit. *We* succeeded, all five of us, by working together.'

'Helluva haul.' Strother spoke quietly, but with elation. 'All those renegades, our prisoners, Bearcat good and dead and, just to sweeten the pot, all the Lucky Seven gold!'

'Not to mention,' Rick reminded him, 'a treacherous sergeant of the Third Cavalry and his five accomplices.'

'Jackpot,' grinned Strother.

'A question, Vin,' said Rick. 'How long do you estimate it will take us to reach Camp Kemp? You've been there, so you'd have some idea. Bear in mind we have many prisoners to transport, their weapons and the gold. And, en route, we have to collect Hake and his sidekicks. You, Roy, Jerry and Bruno have to change out of those uniforms. It will all take time and effort, but think of the effect on the commanding officer.'

'Uh huh,' grunted Strother.

'It's what you've dreamed of,' said Rick. 'To present the army with proof positive that Shay County can function without benefit of martial law.'

'Beautiful,' Strother said with relish. 'Just beautiful.'

'Consider the distance to be travelled,' urged Rick.

'Yeah, I'm thinkin' about that,' nodded Strother. 'How – uh – how're we gonna make this move? You got any notions?'

'With Bruno driving and me manning the Gatling, the wagon can carry no more than the renegades' weapons,' opined Rick. 'Our prisoners, red and white, will make the journey on horseback. We'll distribute those pokes of happy yellow so that riders will carry no more than one. That way, the horses won't be too heavily burdened.'

'Keep talkin',' nodded Strother. 'You're doin' fine.'

'You, Jerry and Bruno will be escorting Hake's party,' said Rick. 'That means you take the lead. Roy and I will follow in the wagon, Roy driving, me manning the Gatling. These renegades will be ordered to ride in a V formation. With me covering them, they'll be in no doubt about their chances of making a run for it. So – Camp Kemp?'

'All right,' said Strother, after some mental calculation. 'We forget about eatin', keep movin' along steady, we'll maybe see Camp Kemp before sundown.'

'Excellent,' said Rick. 'Let's get organized.'

Considering the amount of organization required, it pleased him that they were vacating the box canyon little more than thirty minutes later.

In Shayville, at about the same time the northbound winners and losers were making a brief stop to retrieve six other losers, the lady known as Mrs Elmira Tebbutt found herself face to face with a cavalryman on Main Street.

Hattie decided this soldier could be spared a kick to the shin, a straight right to the jaw or an edge-of-the-hand blow to the Adam's apple. This young man, so plain of face, wore the uniform of an officer and greeted her with the utmost courtesy; she appreciated his respectful salute which, for a moment, made her feel as important as a general's wife.

'Your pardon, ma'am. Do I have the honour of addressing Mrs Elmira Tebbutt?'

'You have, young man. Most kind of you to consider it an honour.'

'Lieutenant Clive Purvis, Mrs Tebbutt. Your

servant.'

'Oh, my! Such gallantry. Third Cavalry regiment, I presume?'

'My superior officer is Major Royle, commandant of the garrison here.'

'Such a pity, Lieutenant.'

'Pardon, ma'am?'

'How much safer the good ladies of this town would feel, were enlisted men of the Third Cavalry as courteous as your good self.'

'I regret …'

'I too, Lieutenant.'

'Quite so. May I inquire, Mrs Tebbutt, if you are free at this time? The major would appreciate a few words with you.'

'Major Royle wishes to see me?'

'If it be convenient to you. Pressure of work, his many responsibilities, prevented his visiting you at your hotel. I'm instructed to escort you to his headquarters. It is, of course, a request and an invitation, not a summons.'

Hattie, always adept at concealing her feelings, resisted the impulse to chuckle, managed to appear no more than curious. So Royle had finally decided to look her over? Fine by her. She had full confidence in her disguise and maintaining the ageing woman speech pattern was never a problem to her. With graphic memories of Royle's reaction to the beauteous and seductive Lucinda, she decided she would enjoy his reaction to Lucinda's dear old mother.

'I accept the invitation,' she smiled.

'By your leave,' said Purvis, offering his arm.

They were eyed curiously by passers-by during their progress to the Grand Hotel. Out and about were several interested locals, two of whom were the Leesons.

'Look, Benjamin,' breathed Chloe.

'Make an odd couple, don't they?' the mayor casually commented. 'Quite a contrast, your friend Mrs Tebbutt and the lieutenant. Couldn't call him handsome, could you? But he seems a nice enough feller.'

'It's only the troopers, the enlisted men, who keep frightening us.'

'Shouldn't you say *used* to frighten you?'

'That's right, yes. No unseemly conduct in the past twenty-four hours. Our cause is just and, thanks to dear Elmira, we're enjoying a measure of success.'

'Chloe, honey, I call that kind of a prim way of saying the troopers don't take kindly to having their snoots bloodied, their ribs dented and their backsides kicked by salty females.'

Watching from the other side of the street, Deputy Billy Grimble indulged in speculation. It appeared the old battle-axe and her escort were headed for the Grand. Did this mean that bonehead Royle had sent for her?

'Wish I could tag along, be there to see it,' he reflected wistfully. 'That'd *really* be something to see, damned if it wouldn't. Royle tries bullyin' her – she gives him some of what the other old gals've been givin' them skirt-chasin' soldier-boys. On him, a busted snoot'd look good.'

As Purvis ushered her into the lobby, Hattie fixed a disapproving eye on troopers loitering there. Two of them, one with an arm in a sling, the other sporting a magnificent shiner, hastily made themselves scarce. She chuckled inwardly. Plainly, they feared she would let go of the lieutenant's arm and let go at *them*.

'Three flights,' Purvis said apologetically as they began climbing. 'Unfortunately, the major's quarters are on the top floor.'

'You're very considerate, Lieutenant,' she murmured. 'But do not concern yourself. I'm in excellent health. I promise you I'll not be huffing and puffing when you present me to the major.'

When they finished their climb and arrived at the door of Royle's suite, Purvis knocked, opened the door, thrust his head inside and announced,

'Mrs Tebbutt, sir.'

He ushered Hattie in, withdrew and closed the door. Royle rose from his desk chair, greeted her affably and invited her to be seated, all the time subjecting her to an intent scrutiny.

'I sincerely appreciate your finding time to accept my invitation, Mrs Tebbutt,' he declared, resuming his chair. 'For me, dear lady, a long-awaited pleasure.'

'And you've been *so* curious.' She smiled teasingly and waggled a finger. 'Wondering, I'm sure. What kind of person must she be? you must have asked yourself. This Tebbutt woman tutoring the female population of Shayville, instructing respectable ladies in the art of self-defence.'

'I must confess – yes – I *have* been curious.'

'And perhaps just a little worried, Major? I'm told the casualty rate is quite alarming, ruffianly troopers in such reduced condition as to be unfit for duty.'

'You have – ahem – enjoyed some measure of success, Mrs Tebbutt. I congratulate you, but may I remind you of my generosity in giving my official permission for your meetings to continue?'

'That *was* generous of you. I'm sure you're a kind man at heart, and assure you my pupils appreciate it.'

He was still studying her and, to her amusement,

becoming quite florid. Was he blushing?

'I perceive,' he said, 'some slight resemblance. I refer, of course, to Miss Tebbutt, your charming daughter Lucinda.'

Her eyebrows rose.

'Lucinda? You and my daughter are on first-name terms?'

'We were immediately attracted to each other,' he declared, grinning eagerly, his teeth flashing. 'Charming is hardly the word, is it? A stunningly beautiful young lady, your daughter. How proud of her you must be.'

'I am indeed,' she assured him. 'I think of her as my own creation. Though, naturally, my late husband collaborated. It was a joint effort, as I'm sure you understand. Although – you are a bachelor, isn't that so? In which case, you may not understand.'

It took Royle all of twenty seconds to rally from the impact of that so sedately voiced statement.

'I felt it important we should meet, dear lady,' he said. 'True, your activities are of concern to me, but I had another reason, a more – to me – personal reason.'

'Yes?' she asked.

'Let me begin by assuring you my intentions toward your daughter are honourable in every way,' he muttered earnestly. 'Lucinda has won my heart, is in my thoughts every waking moment and – uh – at night also. I haven't been sleeping well.'

'Goodness,' said Hattie.

'As an officer and a gentleman, I am formally requesting your permission to court her.'

'I see.'

'Do I have rivals, may I ask? Yes, I suppose I must have. A young lady so outstandingly beautiful, so fascinating ...'

'And intelligent, Major.'

'Intelligent? Oh, yes. Believe me, it was not just her appearance that captured my heart. I am properly conscious of her fine mind, her innate good taste, her attitudes. Conversation with so refined a lady was such a rare pleasure, but so brief. I was extremely disappointed that she had to leave town so soon after we met.'

'Other commitments,' said Hattie. 'Other interests.'

'Other admirers,' he assumed, wincing.

'Not at present. I would know. She always confides in me.'

'I was so profoundly affected, so much in love, Mrs Tebbutt, that I neglected to request an address.'

'You wish to court Lucinda by mail?'

'If you approve, dear lady.'

'She is resident in Denver. I'm sure she'd be delighted to hear from you.'

'You think so?' Royle's pomade was melting again.

'Certain of it,' smiled Hattie. 'So, if you have pencil and paper ...'

'Right here, Mrs Tebbutt, right here.'

In a clear hand, Hattie wrote an address on a sheet of paper and passed it across the desk. Royle scooped it up and held it to his chest. Had she made him a present of $5,000 in $100 bills, he could not have been a happier man. He declared his intention of writing a letter immediately, thanked her again for visiting him, helped her from her chair and ushered her out.

When Major Royle's letter reached its destination, it was bound to cause some confusion. The address Hattie had given him was 538, Dorkin Street, South Denver, the poky office of T.W. Coulter & Son, in service to the gentry of the capital as maintenance experts. Specifically, the maintenance of cess-pools.

Toward sundown of this day, the lookout on duty was gazing boredly southward from his position on the catwalk to the left of the gate in the high stockade wall, the main entrance to Camp Kemp, base of the 3rd Cavalry regiment. The lookout was a long-jawed trooper name of Mulrooney and, in a matter of moments, his boredom would give way to shock.

# 8
# Withdrawal Pains

Trooper Mulrooney never enjoyed sentry duty daytime or night. Nothing to see out there, just miles of flats to the south, a timbered ridge far to the east, mountains to the west, more flatland to the north.

He was at first only mildly curious about the dust rising above the southern horizon. His curiosity increased when it struck him that he was seeing more dust than could be raised by just a couple of riders. So he waited until the riders, all of them, also the wagon, became discernible. He then used his telescope, brought all advancing men and horses into focus – and shook his head dazedly. He made a closer appraisal as the big party drew closer, then began trembling.

Dropping the spyglass, he turned and yelled to a noncom crossing the compound.

'Sarge – get your ass up here – fast!'

Sergeant O'Rorke, six feet two inches of hard-muscled veteran, jerked to a halt, glared up to the south stockade and bellowed a challenge.

'Who said that?'

'Me!'

'Identity yourself, Trooper!'

'Mulrooney!'

Glowering ferociously, O'Rorke beelined for the nearest steps, ascended them three at a time and hurried around to the south lookout post. His first impulse was to seize the trooper by his throat, but he settled for jabbing at his chest with a gnarled forefinger.

'Mulrooney!' he fumed. 'You see these stripes, you know what I am – and what you are? I'm a sergeant. You ain't nothin' but a trooper. Cross me, Mulrooney, and you're in the guardhouse so fast your feet won't touch the ground! Don't you never – *never* – tell me to get my ass *anywhere*!'

'Sarge ...'

'You hearin' me, boy?'

'Hell's sakes, Sarge – *look*!'

Mulrooney pointed. The sergeant glanced southward impatiently, then gaped in disbelief. The big party was coming on steadily, close enough now for him to note such relevant details as a band of demoralized Arapahos, a half-dozen cavalrymen – obviously captives – several civilians, two of them lawmen, a wagon and, in that wagon ...

He whirled and bellowed to a corporal pausing to light his pipe.

'You – Dumfry!'

'Yo, Sarge?'

'Who's duty officer?'

'Captain Markell.'

'Well, by damn, tell the captain to get his ass – I mean ask him to come up here on the double!'

Some seven minutes later, when the square-shouldered and clean-cut Captain Markell entered his private office in the administration building, Colonel Elbert Cobcroft, commanding officer of the

3rd Cavalry, was penning a letter to his daughter and somewhat preoccupied. And not without good cause. His daughter, his beloved Miriam, was contemplating marriage, her suitor an artist, damn it, a portraitist if you please, with a studio in Omaha, doubtless living on the traditional smell of an oilrag, probably in a garret. Did they have garrets in Omaha?

Briskly, the captain made his announcement. Cobcroft, a leathery veteran, shaggy browed with mutton chop sideburns, carefully laid down his pen.

'You said, Captain Markell …?'

'It's true, sir,' said Markell. 'They've arrived. They're in the compound. I have Troops A and E standing by. We're improvising temporary incarceration for the renegades. The county sheriff and three civilians captured them, recovered the Gatling, also the gold seized by Bearcat Webster's braves during the massacre of those prospectors. Webster is dead, killed in a hand-to-hand struggle with a civilian.'

For a long moment, Cobcroft digested this information and fought hard to retain his composure.

'Damnable situation, Captain. Not to mention an embarrassment to the regiment.'

'But most gratifying, surely?' suggested Markell.

'Gratifying? Certainly. But …' Cobcroft grimaced ruefully. 'The shame, Captain, the humiliation. Two of our own men – murdered by a sergeant of this regiment. Three of our own guilty of the theft of the Gatling, the sergeant in league with that blasted renegade Webster. Six traitors of my command apprehended by civilians and a confession obtained by those civilians. How, I ask you, can the Third ever live this down?'

Markell nodded sympathetically and offered consolation.

'In every regiment, sir, and the Third can't hope to be an exception, many of the enlisted personnel are rough types. There'll always be rogue soldiers. It's just too much to expect, in my opinion, that an entire regiment be composed of paragons of virtue.'

'Roughnecks I can cope with,' muttered the colonel. 'But rogues as treacherous as Hake and his accomplices – I'd never have suspected – in all my years in the cavalry ...' He shrugged helplessly. 'Well, you'd best carry on, Captain. When all prisoners have been secured, I'll receive Sheriff Strother and his companions.'

'Hake and the other five are in the guardhouse already,' said Markell. 'The Arapahos have been mustered and are under heavy guard – their spirit is broken anyway. The body of Bearcat Webster?'

'Burial detail,' growled Cobcroft. 'Somewhere *outside* of Camp Kemp, need I stress?'

Within the quarter-hour, extra chairs having been brought in, they were seated with the commandant in his office, Rick, the two lawmen, the blacksmith and the gunsmith. Cobcroft hosted the gathering. Two bottles of his private stock had been broken out and Captain Markell was performing as barkeep; the colonel had also passed out Havana cigars. At his request, Strother began the long explanation; feeling no personal animosity toward Cobcroft, he addressed him courteously.

'Hope you'll understand, Colonel, I couldn't just flop in my office and do nothin'. Hard for a lawman to stay idle – even when martial law's in force – with two heavy crimes hangin' over our heads. For me, it was the massacre at the Lucky Seven claim and the hijackin' of a fortune in gold. For you, it was the hijackin' of a mighty important piece of armoury and

two killin's right here at Camp Kemp. While it's true
the cavalry was investigatin' both crimes …'

'With no success,' scowled Cobcroft. 'Gloat if you
wish, Sheriff Strother. You've earned that right.'

'Be assured, Colonel, my friend Vin's not here to
gloat,' said Rick.

'The sheriff did introduce us,' Cobcroft recalled,
eyeing him thoughtfully. 'Name of Fairchild …?'

'Julius C,' offered Rick.

'Well experienced as an army scout, no youngster
any more, but still formidable it seems,' commented
Cobcroft. 'You found the strength to fight and defeat
that bloodthirsty half-breed. Remarkable, Mister
Fairchild, to say the least.'

'Chuck could've as easily pulled his gun and let
daylight through Bearcat,' grinned Hyatt. 'But he
went at him with his bare hands – and Bearcat slashin'
at him with a knife.'

'Striving for the psychological effect, Colonel,' Rick
modestly explained. 'Bearcat's forces were menaced
by the Gatling, so I anticipated no interference. Of
course, my objective was to subdue Bearcat with my
fists. I felt this would shake his followers, make them
realize he was not the invincible chief they believed
him to be. The knife – well – I had no option, sir. It
had to be a fight to the death.'

'You shoulda heard them Injuns wail,' chuckled
Hyatt.

'The confession made by Trooper Crane.' Cobcroft
frowned at Strother. 'He confessed voluntarily – or
under duress?'

'He blabbed the whole lousy story, so we got all the
answers,' drawled Bass. 'Ain't that what counts?'

'Sir, Trooper Crane has repeated his statement,'
Markell quietly interjected. 'Sergeant Hake's guilt is

clearly established. No doubt Crane hoped for leniency ...'

'The court-martial will make that decision,' muttered Cobcroft. 'As for Hake, he'll face a firing-squad or a gallows.'

'If I may make a point, Colonel,' Rick said politely.

'Speak freely, Mister Fairchild,' nodded Cobcroft. 'You do seem to be the key-figure in this whole affair.'

'Credit where it's due, Colonel,' insisted Rick. 'My discovery of the cached Gatling was purely accidental.'

'A discovery you chose not to report to me, only to the sheriff,' chided Cobcroft.

'Had you been informed, you'd have taken prompt action, I'm sure,' said Rick. 'The Gatling would've been dug up and returned to the Third's armoury.'

'Naturally.'

'But my friend Vin, with due respect for the Third, decided this would leave the job unfinished.'

'Unfinished, Mister Fairchild?'

'We'd still have a mystery unsolved. Who purloined the Gatling and for what purpose? Bearcat was the obvious suspect, until Vin began wondering why the weapon had not been retrieved. Impeded by the dust storm, the hijackers were forced to find a temporary hiding place for the gun. That seemed logical. But it had not yet been retrieved, so Vin decided we should keep the discovery secret, stake out the timber east of the site and apprehend the guilty parties.'

Rick delivered his spiel persuasively, convincing Cobcroft that Strother was a law-officer of greater intelligence than Shay County folk had suspected. During this, Strother somehow contrived to maintain a poker-face. By lying in wait for the hijackers, canny Strother believed he was acting in the best interests of both the civilian population and the 3rd Cavalry. Had he not justified his actions? The Gatling was back where it belonged, Webster too dead to be a threat to anybody, his followers in custody and the Lucky 7 gold recovered. Surely every *i* had been dotted and every *t* crossed?

'Your argument cannot be challenged, Mister Fairchild,' the colonel had to admit.

'Which brings us to the question of whether or not Shayville needs martial law,' said Rick. 'Your pardon, gentlemen. I've been excessively verbose. It would be more appropriate for Vin to make the final point.' He nodded encouragingly to the sheriff. 'In your own words, my friend.'

Strother downed another swig of whiskey, blew a smoke-ring and matched stares with Cobcroft.

'Well, Colonel sir,' he said. 'It wasn't the citizens of our town nor our councilmen that went bellyachin' to the state administration and beggin' for the army to protect 'em. It was the money-men, the bankers of Shayville, just three of 'em.'

'Chicken-livered stuffshirts,' sneered Kilburn.

'My deputies and me, we can keep troublemakin' miners in line,' declared Strother. 'And it's got to where the local ladies can take pretty damn good care of 'emselves. They've learned how to discourage minehands and soldiers too. Yes, sir. Them troopers under Major Royle's command ain't exactly gentlemen, as any Shayville lady'll swear.'

'I'm anticipating your next claim, reading your mind, Sheriff,' sighed Cobcroft.

'Look at it this way,' urged Strother. 'Who got your big gun back? Who got back the stolen gold and handed you Bearcat's whole war party on a platter, along with six of your own soldiers that ain't fit to be soldiers? Major Royle claims he's been investigatin', but did *he* get anywhere?'

'All he's got's a big mouth and a brain so big,' jeered Bass, raising finger and thumb an inch apart.

'We did it all, Colonel,' said Strother. 'One deputy, me and three civilians. Now, if that don't prove Shayville can take care of itself ...'

'Enough, Sheriff Strother, you've made your point,' Cobcroft conceded. 'Tonight, before I retire, I'll draft two statements. The first will rescind Major Royle's orders and will be handed to him by Captain Markell tomorrow morning. On my own initiative, I'm putting an end to martial law in the county seat. The second statement will be addressed to the Defence Department and a copy forwarded to the state administrators. It will explain – satisfactorily I believe – my decision that Shayville no longer requires a garrison force from this regiment to keep the peace.'

'Best news I've heard since Royle's Roughnecks rode in and took over Mayor Leeson's own hotel,' enthused Kilburn.

'You gentlemen will be our overnight guests of course,' said Cobcroft. 'You'll dine in the officers' mess this evening and, when you leave for Shayville in the morning, Captain Markell will accompany you. He'll deliver my message to Major Royle, instructing him to leave the hotel and return to base. It should take an hour at most for all army personnel to withdraw from the township.'

'Hallelujah!' whooped Hyatt.

The victors, upon their return to Shayville at ten o'clock of the following morning, had only one regret. Markell's delivery of the colonel's withdrawal order was an army matter; they could not be present to study Royle's reaction.

And quite a reaction it was. Royle's chagrin was almost comical. Markell and Lieutenant Purvis traded winks, but covertly. For five minutes, Royle stormed about his quarters, shaking his fists, flushed with indignation.

'Is the colonel out of his mind?' he raged.

'You may rely on my discretion, Major,' Markell assured him.

'And mine,' said Purvis.

'We'll forget what you just said,' promised Markell.

'Thunderation!' groaned Royle. 'An order to retreat!'

'Hardly a retreat, Major,' reasoned Markell. 'Your garrison has not been at war with the people of this town.'

'Well ...' began Purvis.

'You were about to say?' prodded Markell.

'Nothing,' decided Purvis.

'To think of all Troop B has done for this town!' seethed the major.

'All that's been done *to* this town,' Purvis dared emphasize.

Fortunately for him, that went over Royle's head.

'And now *this*!' he complained. 'I am ordered back to base, though my work is unfinished, the renegades still at large, the Gatling still missing ...'

'Recovered,' offered Markell.

Royle gaped at him.

'*What* did you say?'

'Recovered,' repeated Markell. 'By the sheriff, one of his deputies and three civilians. Webster's whole band is now under heavy guard at Camp Kemp, his entire force – surrendered – delivered by Sheriff Strother's party, one of whom, an old fellow name of

Fairchild, personally fought and killed Webster. And, for good measure, they also recovered the gold looted from those butchered prospectors. It's all there in the colonel's own hand. You can't have read it very thoroughly.' He consulted his watch. 'That's all, Major. We now have fifty minutes in which to withdraw from Shayville.'

Predictably, the good news had spread throughout town and had been received jubilantly. Shayville folk felt as farming communities do when prayed-for rain signals the end of a long drought. They crowded Main Street's sidewalks when Company B, many of whose personnel were looking much the worse for wear, mounted three abreast. There were no cheers. Memories of the many indignities they had suffered moved the locals to yell such uncharitable comments as,

'Good riddance!'

'Glad to see the last of you skirt-chasin' bums!'

'Git on back where you belong! You ain't needed here!'

'We never did need you!'

'No more'n we need blackwater fever!'

The major's saddled horse was brought to the steps of the Grand Hotel by Captain Markell and Lieutenant Purvis, both mounted. When Royle emerged in full uniform, shoulders squared, moustache bristling, eyes gleaming vindictively, he was loudly jeered. He stood glaring until a mangy dog performed the ultimate parting gesture, padding up to him, cocking a hind leg and urinating on his highly polished boots. The dog received an ovation, Royle's savage kick missed it by three inches and it ambled away with tail wagging.

As Royle began mounting, Deputy Grimble remarked to Deputy Bass,

'Wish I could've got close enough to cut his cinch.

Would that be somethin' or wouldn't it? Him puttin' his boot in his stirrup and goin' down flat on his butt with his saddle on top of him?'

'We oughtn't be greedy, Billy,' grinned Bass. 'You can't have everything.'

The mounted officers moved to the head of the column. It was left to Captain Markell to give the order to move out, Royle's frustration having rendered him temporarily speechless. Along Main the garrison force moved, locals still hurling jibes. From the southern outskirts of the county seat, Company B swung eastward, then northward. Exit the cavalry. Martial law had ended, as had another assignment undertaken by the Braddock Detective Agency.

A northbound stage would make a team change at 3 pm and pick up passengers. At the depot, Rick was informed there were two empty seats. He booked passage in the names of Julius Fairchild and Mrs Elmira Tebbutt, stopped by the Glad Hand to be farewelled by Arlo Coventry and staff, then visited the sheriff's office to join those who had become his allies.

Big Bruno Hyatt was postponing reopening his forge till the morrow. Jerry Kilburn had decided he would not lose much business by staying closed for the rest of this day. He, the blacksmith and Bass were reliving those tense moments at the renegades' hideaway and Vin Strother playing barkeep, refilling glasses from a bottle of good bourbon. Rick was amiably welcomed and offered a shot and a chair.

'Hero of the day, good old Chuck,' grinned Strother. 'Planned all our moves, but gave me the credit.'

'Just being fair, Vin,' shrugged Rick. 'How much

could I have accomplished alone and unaided? Every man did his share, and I'll remember you for that.'

'That sounds kind of final,' frowned Kilburn. 'Aren't thinking of leaving town, are you?'

'We were hopin' you'd settle in Shayville, Chuck,' said Bass.

'You've earned your rest, pal,' Strother said earnestly. 'Listen, I'm not forgettin' what you told us about that – what you learned from Sioux medicine men ...'

'Mental control,' intoned Rick. 'Mind over matter. Conservation of physical strength ...'

'Well, sure,' nodded Strother. 'But you can't keep it up forever. You got to think of the future.'

'You got the savvy of a real young fighter in an old man's body,' warned Hyatt.

'Ah, yes, so true,' agreed Rick. 'But it's too early for me to stagnate, boys. That's what I'd do if I stayed on here. Stagnate. Better I stay on the move for as long as I'm able. So I'm booked on this afternoon's north-bound stage.'

'All the luck, old timer,' offered Kilburn.

'Said you'd remember us,' Bass mumbled sentimentally. 'Well, by damn, it's for sure *we* ain't never gonna forget *you.*'

After three shots of bourbon, Rick felt fine, nowhere near inebriated, quite fit to complete his business with the man who had retained him.

The Leesons had moved back into the Grand Hotel and remustered their staff. Chloe was supervising a full-scale cleaning operation; she had foreseen the need, knowing the billeted troopers to have been an untidy bunch. Rick conferred with the mayor in the comfort of the suite commandeered by the once-bumptious, now chastened, Major Calvin Royle. He accepted a Havana. They lit up and traded grins.

'I can say it now,' declared Leeson. 'That is some hell of a disguise – and the same goes for your fine wife. By the great horned toad, she is sure full of surprises.'

'Depending on your line of work, a man's wife can be the best partner he could hope to have,' said Rick, dropping his old man quaver, reverting to his natural mode of speech.

'You took on a heavy assignment, and damned if you didn't deliver,' Leeson said admiringly. He opened a drawer of his desk and proffered a wad of banknotes. 'You'll find that'll cover your fee, plus expenses, plus a bonus. And no arguments about the bonus. Hell, young feller, you did *so much*.'

Helping himself to pen and paper, writing a receipt, Rick assured him,

'No job is too small, nor too big.'

'Things'll be different from now on,' enthused Leeson. 'The mine bosses finally got wise. Their hired hands'll toe the line in future, we can count on that. Any miner offends any good lady of Shayville, he loses his job and Vin Strother runs him out of the county. That's the right way to keep law and order, son. Relying on our own lawmen, not a gang of hard case soldiers.' As Rick transferred the cash to his wallet, he sighed heavily and told him, 'There's somebody else asked me to convey his thanks. He couldn't thank you personally.'

'Who might that be?'

'John Arnfield, only survivor of the massacre at the Lucky Seven claim. The recovered gold's been converted to cash and the total sum deposited in his bank account. Doc Albertson's operating on him again tomorrow.'

'Tell Arnfield from me he's entirely welcome.'

'If this surgery's successful, he won't need a wheelchair any more. But a cane, yes, the poor feller'll always be lame. Did I say poor? He'll be lame, but rich.'

'So he'll have no financial problems. I'm glad for him, Ben.'

'I'm glad for him too.' Leeson waxed wistful. 'Good man, Arnfield. My guess is, when he's paid his medical expenses, he'll have a stonemason make fine headstones for the graves of his six partners.'

The Braddocks, still appearing to the citizens of Shayville as the aged Mr Fairchild and the almost as aged Mrs Tebbutt, lunched together and mutually agreed they had chalked up another success. Because other diners were in earshot, they resisted the urge to revert to their normal speech patterns.

'I have only one grouch,' Hattie quietly confided.

'Which is ...?'

'We're stuck with these roles till we get home.'

'Can't be helped.'

'Of course not. We can hardly board the stage as our real selves. Too much confusion. "Who are they?" people will wonder. "Where did *they* come from – and how did they get here?" My point is – Mister Julius Fairchild – our character-change trick is too vital to our business to be publicized.'

'You're right, but I resent it. Separate rooms at overnight stops all the way from here to Denver.'

Hattie sighed in mock frustration.

'The things we do for the business we're in.'

At 2.50 that afternoon, when Rick and Hattie boarded the stage, a sizeable representation of appreciative locals were there to bid them goodbye, Vin Strother and his deputies, the Leesons and no fewer than fifteen women who, thanks to the tutoring of Elmira Tebbutt, were now expert at wreaking havoc on troublesome males of the species; it augured ill for any husbands taking too much for granted.

The women cheered as, right on time, the coach rolled off along Main Street.

Rick, seated beside his wife, sized up the other passengers. Introductions were exchanged and he feared the worst – a boring trip. How much stimulating conversation could he expect from four such humourless fellow travellers, two married couples, an austere Methodist minister and his thin, hatchet-jawed spouse, a taciturn farmer and his wife bound for a town some distance north to attend the wedding of their son?

He hated being bored, knew Hattie was hating it too. Their Shayville assignment had been at times amusing, but just as often nerve-wracking and downright perilous. After all they'd achieved, didn't they deserve to relax? And, to either Braddock, relaxation equated with a few laughs, a jest or two, some leg-pulling just for the hell of it. They had been too serious too long. Brilliant investigators they had undoubtedly become but, at heart, they were still showfolk, role-players, performers to whom "dull" was a dirty word.

Rick went into his act four miles later; he couldn't take any more of the grim silence maintained by the other couples, and was sure Hattie was just as bored.

Turning, he studied her intently and, in his old man voice, declared.

'Gad, madam, you're a toothsome dish if ever I saw one.'

'Sir, are you addressing me?' frowned "Mrs Tebbutt".'

The clergyman's mouth set in a hard line. His wife sniffed in disapproval, as did the farmer's wife.

'Addressing you in profound admiration, dear lady,' replied Rick. 'Fairchild's the name. Your servant. Nay! Your slave. Call me Julius, I beg you. By thunder, just sitting beside you makes me feel fifty again.'

'See here, sir ...' began the minister.

'My name is Elmira Tebbutt,' Hattie said curtly. 'I am a respectable widow.'

'Listen, mister, this's no way to behave,' chided the farmer.

Ignoring the other passengers, Rick ogled Hattie.

'A widow?' he exclaimed. 'Great! Who cares if you're respectable? What matters is that you're single and edible – I mean eligible. Little slip of the tongue there. But then you really are a toothsome dish, yes indeed.'

'Such unseemly presumption!' protested the minister's wife.

'Please don't be concerned on my account,' said Hattie. 'This happens all the time. I'm used to it.'

'You mean,' challenged Rick, 'I have rivals? Other men have lost their hearts to you?'

'I can never understand why,' frowned Hattie. 'After all, it's not as though I'm young and beautiful.'

'To me, you'll *always* be young and beautiful.' Rick was now resorting to heavy breathing, to the consternation of the farmer's wife. 'Be warned, Elmira. I'm a man of passion!'

'*Sir!*' gasped the minister.

'If I can't have you, no other man will – I won't permit it!' said Rick. 'Be mine, my love! Marry me and make me the happiest man on earth!'

'Oh, well ...' said Hattie, with a fine show of exasperation. 'I suppose I'll have to say yes, otherwise it'll be nag, nag, nag, mile after mile.'

'Merciful heavens!' gasped the minister's wife. 'You're accepting the proposal of a stranger – a madman?'

'His condition may be curable,' shrugged Hattie. 'Don't worry about me. I'm one of a long line of optimists.' Of Rick she enquired: 'When do you want to marry me?'

'How about the next stop?' he eagerly suggested.

'Oh, very well,' she sighed. 'If you're in that much of a hurry.'

While the passengers gawked in disbelief, Rick whispered in his wife's ear.

'Enjoying the trip, honey?'

'Enjoying the show too,' she softly replied. 'The opening was – well – too bad we're playing to such a dull audience.'

'It was a *great* opening,' he argued.

'Well, at least we won their attention,' she conceded. 'Got any ideas for a big finish? I don't care if they don't applaud, but it'd be fun to shock them right out of their seats.'

'I'll think of something,' Rick promised.